The Snow Blossom

Few people have lived and died more obscurely than the late nineteenth century French girl, Thérèse Martin, yet within a few years of her death she was one of the most famous and beloved women in the world, known to millions of admirers as the Little Flower.

In this novel, based entirely on recorded events and conversations, we follow the career of the obstinate little girl who decided when she was only three that she was going to be a saint and out of whose struggles came the 'Little Way' which still inspires many today. Her story is told against the background of her loving, middle-class family and the contrasting starkness of the enclosed life she struggled to follow. As favourite daughter, unhappy schoolgirl, excited pilgrim, or nun trying to discipline her faults, she remained always a rare and original being whose mission of love remains valid a hundred years later.

Maureen Peters

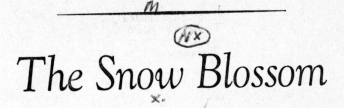

The Snow Blossom

ROBERT HALE · LONDON

© Maureen Peters 1980
First published in Great Britain 1980

ISBN 0 7091 7839 5

Robert Hale Limited
Clerkenwell House
Clerkenwell Green
London EC1R

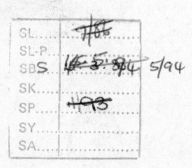
Printed in Great Britain by
Clarke, Doble & Brendon Ltd,
Plymouth and London

PROLOGUE

1872

It was going to be a white Christmas. From time to time Zélie Martin glanced up from her lace making at the flakes of snow whirling beyond the window. Although it was still mid afternoon it was already growing quite dim. Very soon she would have to put away the delicate eye straining work and light the lamp. Louis would be on his way home from the jeweller's shop within the hour and he liked to see the lamp shining in the dark window before he reached the end of the street.

Dear Louis! Zélie's lips curved into an almost maternal smile when she thought of her husband. Although he was seven years her senior, she often fancied that a part of him had never grown up but had remained an eager, rather solemn schoolboy. He had struck her as looking young for his years the very first occasion she had seen him, and on that occasion as he drew aside politely to let her pass him on the bridge, she had known too that she was going to marry him. She had known it as clearly as if the words had been spoken aloud in her head, and been so startled that she had turned round to stare at the tall, dark haired man and found him turned around and staring at her.

Marriage was not in Zélie's scheme of life at all. She had made up her mind when she was quite small that she wanted to be a nun and had kept herself from all emotional entanglements. It had been the most bitter disappointment of her life when the Mother Superior to whom she had presented herself for interview had told her bluntly that she had no vocation. Zélie had hoped so much to become a Sister of St Vincent de Paul that the shock had left her too numb with disappointment to plead her case further, and she had walked home in the pouring rain without remembering to put up her umbrella. She had made no further attempts to enter a religious order, but had remained quietly at home with her father, running his household and building up a little circle of clients, for she made lace with such skill.

It had been several months before she had seen him again and on that occasion it had seemed quite natural for them to fall into conversation. His name was Louis Martin and he had a jeweller's shop at the other side of Alençon. What interested her more was that he too had applied to enter a religious order and been as firmly rejected as herself.

"So now I wait to see what destiny the good Lord has in store for me," he had said.

Zélie was already quite certain that their destinies were joined, but it had taken months for him to work up to a proposal and even then there had been a reluctance in his manner as if he were acting against his own inclinations.

She had understood why on their wedding night when, the excitement of the service and the family celebration behind them, she had sat up in bed in her new, lace-trimmed nightgown and heard him say,

"We will keep our desire for chastity and live together as brother and sister."

It had taken months to change his mind about that too, and she had had to be subtle in persuading him that if they wished to have children for the glory of God then something more than a goodnight kiss on the brow was required. Even after that he always insisted that they prayed together before and after the act of love, asking for children to be born. 'And God was certainly listening,' Zélie thought with

6

wry humour as she rose to tidy her work away. Eight babies in thirteen years was an abundant answer to prayer, even though four of them had gone swiftly back to Heaven. Her two little boys had lived for only a few months each and then Hélène, who was four years old, had fallen sick of consumption and died. That had been a bitter time, for Hélène had been a bright prattling little girl just beginning to be interesting, and Zélie had been worn out with nursing her, through the nausea of another pregnancy. It had annoyed her very much when a neighbour had said in tones of well meant sympathy, "Now that poor Hélène is gone, the new babe will fill her space."

"As if I were a bird who couldn't count her eggs!" Zélie said indignantly to Louis.

The new babe Mélanie, had occupied her own space in the household for just three months and then slipped away like a tiny wingless angel.

Fortunately the four surviving girls had outgrown the perilous years of babyhood and were her great joy.

Lighting the lamp she thought of them with affectionate longing. Marie was nearly thirteen and already quite a young lady, and Pauline, at eleven, was going to be a beauty with her long hair and flawless complexion. They would be home soon from their boarding school at Le Mans, bringing with them nine-year-old Léonie.

Zélie frowned, thinking anxiously of her third daughter who was clumsy and slow, with none of Marie's liveliness or Pauline's good sense. Poor Léonie had wept bitterly and begged not to be sent away to school, but Zélie had hardened her heart and disengaged the child's clinging hands. At school Léonie would learn to live with other children, and not give way to the screaming tantrums in which she indulged whenever her will was thwarted.

Zélie couldn't avoid a little pang of guilt for it had to be admitted that, with only Céline at home, it was peaceful and serene. At three Céline was a grave, sedate little person who spoke earnestly of the new baby that would be arriving after Christmas. Céline was longing for a baby sister and Zélie suspected the wish would be granted. She was carrying this child all to the front as she had carried the other girls, and she was feeling remarkably well. Her appetite was good, her sleep tranquil, and with her tiny frame modestly swathed in a shawl of her own making, she looked younger than her forty-three years.

The snow was falling faster now, piling up in the corner of the sills. Zélie hoped Louis would have the sense to take a cab home. There was really no need for him to go down to the shop at all for he had virtually retired from the business since the death of her father had left them comfortably provided. She herself only continued to make lace because the occupation itself was a pleasure to her.

Glancing about the modest parlour with its Turkey rug and lovingly polished furniture, its books and ornaments, and glowing fire, she felt contentment settle over her like a mantle. There was no denying that her way had been set in pleasant places.

Hastily, lest contentment degenerate into smugness, she took the "Lives of the Martyrs" from the bookcase and settled down to read, shielding her face from the heat of the fire with her hand. Apart from the cracking of wood in the grate and the plash-plash of the snow beyond the uncurtained window the room was silent and peaceful.

The pain came suddenly, tearing at her shoulder with such ferocity that she dropped the book and sprang up, crying out in agony. Despite the warmth of the room, she was as cold as if she had been plunged into a bath of ice cold water, and with the cold came wave after wave of overwhelming evil, unlike anything she had ever experienced before. Whirling about she stood facing the invisible evil, her legs shaking and tears of pain coursing down her face.

Then, slowly and shiveringly, she raised her hand to make the sign of the cross. Gradually the intense cold and the pervading sense of evil ebbed away and she bent to pick up her fallen book, clutching it tightly as if it were a talisman.

All her life she had prided herself on her good sense and level head, but now she felt suddenly as forlorn as a small child lost in a wilderness of space and darkness, with no comforting hand to guide her back to the light.

Within her the child leapt and kicked. She put her hand on her swollen stomach and stood, waiting for the rapid beating of her heart to subside. Louis would be coming soon when the recent incident could be discussed and he, with his simple faith in the essential goodness of existence, would quieten her fears. The room was warm again now and her sense of being watched and mocked was gone.

This child must be a very special one, Zélie reflected, for the forces of evil to attack her with such violence just before its birth. She wondered if, after all these years, their prayers might be answered and a healthy son conceived.

ONE

Louis Martin had finished his correspondence for the day and put the letters into a neat pile, ready for posting. The sun poured through the window, patterning the carpet with lozenges of gold, and for a few minutes he relaxed, enjoying the warmth of it. There were few occasions in these troubled days when he allowed himself a brief respite from his cares.

The house itself was become a place of hushed footsteps and lowered voices, with straw laid down outside the door so that the rattling of wheels over the cobbles wouldn't disturb the invalid. Soon he would go up into the bedroom, with its clutter of medicine bottles and lowered blinds, to sit with Zélie for a while. She had deprived herself of the company of the two youngest girls, telling him,

"I don't want Céline and Thérèse to remember me as a moaning, dying mother."

The two oldest girls were mature enough to help with the nursing and both Marie and Pauline were diligent in their duties. Léonie was the greatest anxiety to him, for at thirteen she had not outgrown her childish tantrums, the fits of brooding sullenness that descended upon her without warning and were impossible to lift. Yet he must remember that Léonie could also be good natured. Only the previous week she had put all her little dolls and their clothes into a basket and told the little ones to choose what they wanted.

Céline, after due consideration, had taken a roll of silk braid, whereupon Thérèse had snatched the entire basket shouting, "I choose everything!"

Louis's frown was an indulgent one. Everything that his youngest child did or said seemed to him to be touched with magic. It had been like that ever since her birth, and it pained him when Zélie corrected her.

"We are fortunate that the poor child survived at all," he had said once in gentle reproof.

She had been a tiny scrap of a thing with enormous eyes and a feeble wailing cry, and Zélie had been unable to feed her. It was by the grace of Providence that Rose Taillé, a farmer's wife of their acquaintance, had had milk enough for two, and had taken the ailing mite into her own home at Sémallé for the first year. The whole family had gone out regularly to see her and to rejoice as the thin, fretful baby grew plump and rosy, gurgling with pleasure when her parents bent over her cot, or being held on the broad back of La Rousse, the Taillé family cow, as it ambled slowly around the field.

Before she was a year old she had been weaned and brought back to Alençon. Louis had thought her a remarkable baby, already pulling herself upright on sturdy little legs and lisping her first words. She was a strong-willed child too, beating her tiny fists on the tray of her high chair when she wanted attention and yelling until she was red in the face if she was refused a second helping of dessert.

"We must be careful not to indulge all her whims," Zélie had said.

Easy to say but not so easy to keep one's resolve, Louis thought, for Thérèse was so bright and affectionate that it was hard to bring oneself to scold her. Little as she was she already had a lively sense of contrition, saving up her small naughtinesses to confess to him when he arrived home at night. There had been the occasion when, having

12

amused herself by pulling the corners of the wallpaper away from the wall, she had tugged anxiously at Zélie's skirt, whispering, "Tell Papa about the paper. Tell him how wicked I've been."

But there was no denying that she could be obstinate. There were times when nothing in the world would induce her to give way and admit that she was wrong. Zélie had even sent her down to sit in the cellar, expecting that within the hour Thérèse would be begging to be allowed out.

"Not a bit of it!" Zélie had told him. "The little madam sat there all the day long and was quite prepared to stop down there all night as well. In the end I was the one who had to give in. I tried to bribe her the other day with a sou, telling her she could have it if she would kiss the ground but she refused quite indignantly."

Louis had felt a sneaking sympathy for his little daughter. Children hated having their dignity diminished, and Thérèse, for all her mischief, had an air about her that in his fondness he thought of as almost royal. When they were alone together he lavished endearments on her, calling her his little princess, his white flower, his pet. Of the five girls she was undoubtedly his favourite, the Benjamin of his heart. Fortunately her sisters loved her dearly otherwise there might well have been jealousy to combat.

There was a tap on the door and Pauline entered. He looked up at the tall fifteen year old with pleasure, seeing in her quiet features some indication of the strong-minded woman she was to become. Her long plaits were wound about her head and her expression was, as usual, gravely composed.

"May I talk to you, Papa?" she enquired.

"Of course, my love, but I must go up to your poor mother soon, and the little ones will be in."

"Céline and Thérèse went to the park with Madame

Leriche, and Mamma is asleep," Pauline said, sitting down on a high backed chair and folding her hands primly in her lap. "Marie and Léonie are baking bread for tomorrow."

"How neatly you organize everything!" he said gratefully.

"Mamma is not going to get better, is she?" Pauline said abruptly.

"The growth was far too advanced," Louis said heavily. "A week or a few days—the doctor has warned me to expect no miracles.'

"Arrangements will have to be made," Pauline said, folding her lips against pain. "When Mamma has gone, will we stay on here in Alençon? Wouldn't it be wiser to start afresh in a place where there are no sad memories?"

"I have talked the matter over with your mother," Louis said. "This town house is too cramped for all of us and the little ones need a garden to run about in. Your mother feels it would be a good idea for us all to move to Lisieux. We would be near your Uncle Isidore then, and Thérèse and Céline would have playmates in Jeanne and Marie."

He sighed as he spoke for his wife's brother, Isidore Guérin, was a somewhat domineering character with a prosperous chemist's business and a fashionable wife. He frequently travelled to Paris and Geneva for medical conferences and, despite his kindness of heart, had never succeeded in hiding his conviction that his sister might have done better for herself.

"And Lisieux is a very agreeable town with some charming countryside around it," Pauline said. "You could open your business there, Papa, and have some occupation to fill the hours."

"You are so remarkably like your mother," Louis commented.

Zélie had always treated him as if he were a beloved but

14

slightly backward child, who would get into mischief if his hands were not supplied with tasks to keep them busy. It looked as if Pauline were planning to step into Zélie's shoes.

"Would you and Marie like to go to Lisieux to live near your cousins?" he enquired.

"We would both like it very much," Pauline said, her serious face brightening. "There are some elegant houses on the outskirts of the town. Couldn't you afford one of those, Papa, if you were to sell this house?"

"It could be arranged." He checked his pleasure and looked at her a little guiltily. "But we mustn't stop praying for a miracle for your mother."

"She made pilgrimage to Lourdes and there was no miracle," Pauline said. "I think she is resigned to her death now and only wanted to be certain that we will be looked after."

"Your mother is a saint," Louis said, crossing himself.

"There is something else, Papa." Her tone had altered and there was tenseness in her fingers as they gripped one another.

"Yes, my dear?"

"I will be sixteen next month," Pauline said, "and no longer a child."

"Indeed, no! You and Marie are both young ladies now," he said bracingly. "Soon you will be thinking of young men, I daresay, and I will have to beat them from the door with a stick."

"It is not my wish to take an earthly husband," Pauline said. "No, let me tell it, Papa, before you say anything. Mamma told me how, long ago, she wished to become a nun, but God had other plans for her. I have always tried to be like Mamma in every possible way."

"And succeeded admirably," he said.

"It seems to me that I have inherited many of her wishes," Pauline said. "I want to enter the religious life as she wanted to do. 'Want' is the wrong word—I have never thought of doing anything else but become a nun."

"Of St Vincent de Paul?"

"No. I want to enter Carmel," Pauline said.

"An enclosed Order! My dear child, you are far too young to make up your mind on such an important matter."

"Too young to enter," Pauline said calmly, "but not too young to make up my mind. There is a Carmel at Lisieux and eventually I hope to be accepted as a postulant there."

"Eventually?" His expression became more hopeful.

"I couldn't think of leaving you, Papa, for several years yet," Pauline said. "Marie cannot be left alone to act as housekeeper when Mamma has gone, so there is no question of my taking up my vocation until I am of age. You will not refuse your consent?"

"If you are still determined in—let us say five years—I will bestow my blessing upon you freely." he promised.

"You're very kind, Papa," she said, "and I do beg pardon for having brought up the matter at such a time, but I have confided in Mamma already."

"You didn't upset her, did you?" he asked sharply.

"She was delighted with my decision," Pauline said. "I think she has always hoped that one of us would fulfil her own ambition, but she is pleased that I will be staying with the family for a few years."

"You are the mainstay of the family," Louis said. "You and Marie have made my burdens so much easier these past months."

"I wish there was more to be done for Mamma," Pauline said, rising from her place. "She is in the most terrible pain and the medicine only makes her sick."

"The doctor promised to call in again this evening, and

16

I must go and sit with Mamma for a while," Louis said.

"Why don't you take a little walk and post your letters?" Pauline suggested. "You have been indoors all day, Papa. We cannot have you getting sick too."

"Well, I really don't know." He hesitated, tempted by the sunshine. It was not poor Zélie's fault, of course, but the sickroom had a sweet, cloying, airless scent that depressed him.

"You might meet the little ones and save Madame Leriche from having to escort them all the way home," Pauline said slyly.

"In that case, I might as well slip out," he said thankfully. "You will sit with Mamma? She likes to have someone there when she wakes."

"Yes, of course."

She handed him his hat and stick and waited patiently while he wound a scarf around his throat. Despite the August heat Louis was always nervous of taking cold. A walk would do him good, and though she would not hurt him for the world by saying so his presence in the sickroom fretted her mother dreadfully, for he continually implored her to assure him that she was feeling a little better.

Outside Louis squared his shoulders and took a long, satisfying breath of fresh air. La Rue de Saint Blaise was dedicated to the patron of sore throats and he believed that his own delicate throat was improving. It was necessary for him to retain his health more than ever now that poor Zélie was dying and he would soon be left with five motherless girls to rear.

Pauline had been right in advising him to move to Lisieux. The house in the steep, cobbled street held too many memories of the life he and Zélie had shared. It had been a good marriage despite his initial reluctance to become involved with a purely human love, and though he had forsworn the vow of chastity made in his boyhood he hoped that the size of his family was a measure of the Lord's forgiveness. It had been a holy marriage, he thought, with he and Zélie rising at five-thirty each morning to attend Mass and reading aloud from some devotional book for an hour or so in the evening. The only recreation he ever allowed himself was an afternoon's fishing and the whole of his catch was always delivered to the local Poor Clare convent.

No! There would be too many reminders of Zélie in Alençon. Better to sell up and move to Lisieux.

Pleased to have reached a decision he strode on, occasionally pausing to exchange a brief word with some sympathetic enquirer. Neighbours had been so kind since Zélie's illness had begun, sending fruit and flowers and little delicacies to tempt her appetite, volunteering to look after the children, never passing the shop without looking in to ask how she was.

"Papa! Papa!"

An eager little voice shrilled from the other side of the road, interrupting his musing. Madame Leriche, resplendent in her new feathered hat, had paused holding the hands of her two charges more firmly, but although Céline had waited obediently, Thérèse was already tugging her hand free. A moment later, and she was across the road and flinging herself into his arms.

"Papa! We saw you coming! Céline and me—we saw you!"

He hugged her tightly, pleased by her pleasure. She was surely the prettiest child that he had ever seen, her face rosy, her long fair curls peeping from beneath her straw bonnet, her blue eyes sparkling. She was wearing a blue dress ruched at the hem, with a little jacket to protect her arms from sunburn, and she looked delicious enough to

18

eat. He nuzzled her ear and set her on her feet again as Madame Leriche crossed towards him with Céline in tow.

"Monsieur Martin, I hope Madame Martin is not worse," Madame Leriche said.

"She is sinking," he answered in a low voice, but Thérèse's quick ear had caught the words.

"Is Mamma gone to Heaven yet?" she enquired.

"Not yet, my love, but very soon." He pressed her hand against his side and gave Madame Leriche an eloquent look.

"It is a very, very sad affair," the good lady said, shaking her head.

"It is God's Will," he answered.

"And God is almighty," Madame Leriche said piously.

"What does that mean, Papa?" Céline asked, looking up at him enquiringly.

"I know what 'almighty' means!" Thérèse shouted, jumping up and down. "It means that He can do anything He likes!"

The elders exchanged indulgent smiles over her head. "Have the children been good?" Louis enquired.

"Good as gold," Madame Leriche said promptly. "It is a pleasure to have them at my house."

"We are most grateful for your help," he assured her.

"Anything that I can do, you must never hesitate."

"Ah, when trouble comes, one is aware of the goodness of friends," he said. "Come, children. Say goodbye to Madame Leriche."

"Goodbye, Madame Leriche, and thank you for having us both," they chorused obediently.

Turning homeward, having slipped the letters into the mailbox, Louis watched the two of them as they walked ahead of him. Céline's head was inclined towards her smaller sister and they were chattering but, as they drew near the house, their footsteps slowed, the chatter dwindling into silence.

"Mamma is very sick, isn't she?" Céline said, turning to look at him.

"Very sick indeed," he answered gravely.

"Mamma is going to Heaven," Thérèse said. "She will be able to do anything she likes when she gets there."

"We will all go to Heaven one day if we are good," Louis said, never averse to pointing a moral.

"I am going to be very good and do everything that God wants," Thérèse announced. "Then I'll go to Heaven and God will do everything I tell Him."

"I hardly think so——" Louis began, but Marie was at the front door calling,

"Papa! Papa, we think you should send for the doctor at once. Mamma has taken a turn for the worse."

"Go up to your room," he told the little ones, and to his relief they went at once, not asking questions but scurrying up the stairs without a backward look.

"Do you think they will let us see Mamma before she goes?" Thérèse enquired as they were taking off their jackets and bonnets.

"It's only her soul that goes," Céline said. "Her body is put into the ground for flowers to grow."

Thérèse was silent, frowning slightly. Although she had been told over and over that Mamma was soon going to Heaven, the event had no reality for her. Heaven was up in the sky where she had already seen the inital of her name pricked out in stars. It was all very well for Papa to tell her that it was part of the constellation of Orion. She was quite certain that her name was written in Heaven already.

"We won't go unless we do good deeds," Céline said.

Thérèse fumbled in her pocket and brought out a length of knotted string. Each knot represented a good deed and,

20

at the end of the day, she counted them on her fingers and told God the total. She made another knot carefully. The ham that Madame Leriche had given them for dinner had been too salty, but she had eaten it without complaint.

"The doctor is here," Céline announced, peering down into the street.

"Let me see him!"

The doctor was a genial man who could produce sugar mice out of his top hat. Thérèse struggled up to the window ledge but the street was deserted, the closing of the door below signalling his entry.

"Let's go down and see him!" She jumped down to the floor.

"He will be busy tending Mamma," Céline said. "Anyway we were told to stay here."

Thérèse having no argument to offer, gave her sister a shove, and stuck out her lower lip.

"Now you'll have to undo your good deed knot and I won't talk to you again," Céline cried indignantly.

"Not ever?" Thérèse, untying the knot, looked at her sister with interest. "Won't you talk to me when we're both old ladies? Won't you talk to me when we're both dead and in Heaven?"

"Oh, you are silly, Thérèse!" Céline cried, laughing in exasperation. "I don't know what on earth you'll grow up to be if you're as silly as this now!"

"I shall grow up to be a saint," Thérèse said, trying to balance on one leg and wobbling precariously.

Céline giggled, and Thérèse stopped her balancing act and surveyed the bigger child warily. Then, pulling out the string again, she tied another knot in it, saying, "That's for not smacking you!"

"Girls, make less noise," Marie scolded, putting her head in at the door. "Léonie will give you your supper and put

21

you to bed. We shall be very busy downstairs."

She had gone before they could ask any questions, and instinctively they drew closer together, their eyes filled with apprehension. Mamma would be leaving very soon, they guessed, and they had no part in the farewells. When Léonie came upstairs with their supper tray she found them sitting side by side on the big double bed they shared, their small faces tense.

"You are to say your prayers for me tonight," Léonie said. "Papa has said you must go to bed early and be very good."

They would have preferred to stay downstairs, but Léonie, at thirteen, was bigger than they were and quite capable of slapping them if they argued.

The long evening drew into darkness, punctuated by the sound of hushed voices and footsteps below. They had said their prayers and Papa had looked in to blow them a kiss and gone away again without saying anything. Léonie had tiptoed out and the lamp cast queer shadows against the wall.

Thérèse was shaken out of a dream in which she had been chasing two hideous little demons in and out of the linen room. It was still dark, but Pauline stood, candle in hand, urging them to get up and dress quickly because the priest was come to give Mamma the Last Rites before she set out on her heavenly journey.

It was not as Thérèse had imagined it would be. There was no singing and not a glimpse of an angel, only the dimly lit sickroom, with clouds of pungent incense drifting about the bed on which Mamma was propped up, with her skeleton thin fingers outside the white coverlet.

They knelt in order of age, hands clasped, with Thérèse at the end of the row. Her eyes, wide and blue and still clouded by nightmare, were riveted on the bed. Mamma had always been so brisk and lively, never idle, for even when she sat down she had her lace work in her hands. The gaunt frame on the bed didn't look like Mamma at all but like some dreadful, yellowing wax doll.

She knelt for a long time, her small fingers numbed by the dawn chill, and then someone put the sheet over Mamma's face and Papa began to cry very loudly and painfully, with Marie clinging to him and weeping as well.

The doctor touched Thérèse gently on the shoulder and she rose and went out into the hall. There was a long, shiny box propped up against the wall. She had not noticed it on the way down, but now she looked up at it and knew what it was without being told.

Her sisters were being ushered out and the door of the sickroom closed, muffling Papa's sobs.

Léonie, her face ugly with grief, said on some impulse of cruelty, "Mamma is dead! You haven't got a mother now."

"Marie will be my mother," Céline said promptly.

"And Pauline will be mine!" Thérèse flung herself into the older girl's arms.

"We'd better take the little ones back to bed," Marie said, drying her eyes on a corner of her apron.

As they mounted the stairs Thérèse looked back through the banisters and saw Léonie all by herself, staring forlornly at the coffin.

TWO

Les Buissonets was, in the family's opinion, a great improvement on their previous home. It was a handsome red brick house, with white woodwork, standing well back from the Trouville road in a secluded garden planted thickly with laurel and ivy. At the top of the house an ornate belvedere with wide, curving windows provided a retreat for Louis. The other apartments were sufficiently spacious, comfortably furnished with carved mahogany tables and chairs, sofas and high backed armchairs padded with horsehair, ornaments from the shop and new, patterned carpets.

It had been good of Isidore to find a place for them so quickly and to have helped with all the arrangements. Although he was eighteen years younger than his brother-in-law he was far more worldly wise, advising Louis where the best site for a new shop would be and introducing him to neighbours of good social standing.

"For we have seven daughters between us to be married off, my friend!" Isidore had said in the booming voice that made poor little Thérèse so nervous. "We had better establish our social connections at once."

Louis had said nothing. The prospect of his daughters marrying and being forced to endure the intimacies of wedlock made him anxious. Fortunately Pauline was still quietly bent upon entering Carmel as soon as she attained her majority and, though Marie occasionally spoke of getting married one day, no threatening suitor had yet darkened the horizon. They were both excellent daughters, sharing the duties of the household between them, with Céline deferring to Marie in everything and little Thérèse taking Pauline as her model. His greatest worry was Léonie who, at nearly seventeen, still showed traces of the screaming rages that had disfigured her childhood. She was an odd, sullen creature, apt to lavish affection on the little ones at one moment and to scold them vehemently the next. Louis supposed there had to be a problem child in every family, but he wondered what made Léonie so different from her bright, graceful sisters. Again it was Isidore who had proposed a solution.

"The poor girl is far too temperamental for Marie and Pauline to handle. Let her go as a boarder to the Abbey where she can be with companions of her own age."

The Abbey school was run by the Benedictine nuns and Léonie had been settled there now for over a year. She seemed happy enough there, though her teachers warned him not to expect too much in the way of scholastic attainment.

"The child is retarded in both reading and writing," the headmistress had said, "and she has severe emotional problems. In another family she might very well have been hidden away."

The idea of hiding away one of his beloved daughters had shocked Louis immeasurably, but he had to admit that life was far more tranquil without her disturbing presence. Deep down he confessed that it was more tranquil without Zélie too. She had been a splendid wife and her loss had saddened him deeply, but there was no denying that her chief virtue for him had lain in her ability to bear him children. He could love his daughters unreservedly without any fleshy desires marring the purity of his affection. Zélie, with her hair loose and her shoulders bare, had roused in him feelings that left him shamed and confused.

Life at Les Buissonets was both tranquil and ordered. He still rose for Mass at six o'clock and, unless he had business in town, spent the morning up in the belvedere where he could read and write in peace. After dinner he would take Thérèse for her walk, always spending a few minutes in church with his small daughter kneeling beside him, upright with hands folded and eyes screwed shut as Pauline had taught her. It was Pauline too who gave her lessons in reading and writing and, upon their return from the walk, insisted that she do a little sewing before she was allowed into the garden.

On warm evenings Louis would sit there watching the tiny figure in the blue smock as it dug and weeded assiduously in the plot of garden set aside for her, or built shaky little altars out of pretty stones and bits of twig. She was also fond of making concoctions of seeds and grasses which she called medicines and presented to him solemnly to pretend to take. Every action of hers struck him as charming and even her little naughtinesses had about them an innocence he found impossible to scold.

"You will ruin her," Zélie had warned, but Zélie had been stricter with the children than he himself could bring himself to be.

He smiled reflectively as the echo of the children's voices came to him faintly from below. Céline and Thérèse got on so well together that he often pitied Isidore whose own daughters frequently argued.

In the bedroom Céline, a ruler in her hand, was being schoolmistress to a row of dolls. More dolls sat with their faces turned to the wall and paper cones on their heads and it was at these that Thérèse was looking with sympathy.

"Why do my children always get put in the corner?" she asked.

"Because they're always naughty," Céline said.

"They're only naughty because you make them be naughty," Thérèse pointed out.

"I make them be naughty to match you," Céline said.

"I'm not naughty!" Thérèse exclaimed.

"Who called Victoire a nasty brat?" Céline countered.

"That was because she wouldn't reach out her great long arm and fetch down a candlestick for me from the mantel-shelf. She ought to have obliged me."

"And Papa says we must always treat servants with great kindness and respect."

"Well, I did apologize," Thérèse reminded her, "and I shall confess it next time I go."

"Much use you confessing!" Céline said scornfully. "Why, the priest can't even see you when you're there!"

Thérèse blushed scarlet. To her great chargin she was still so tiny that even when she stood in the confessional box her head didn't reach the grille, and the priest, puzzled by the voice that apparently came from nowhere, had come round to see if anybody was actually there.

"I can't help being little," she said defensively. "It's on account of my age. You're mean to say things like that!"

"Then you won't want to play with me any more, will you?" Céline said nastily. "I won't be schoolteacher one minute longer—and I won't play anything else either."

"Wouldn't you like to play House?" Thérèse coaxed. "You could be the Mamma and I will be your darling daughter."

"You're not my darling daughter," Céline said flatly. "You're a little nuisance."

"I'd smack you for that," Thérèse said with dignity, "but it's against my rule of life."

"You're too little to have a rule of life," Céline said loftily, gathering up her dolls and preparing to depart.

"I am not so! I've had a rule of life ever since I was a baby," Thérèse said.

"Ever since you were a baby!" Céline echoed. "Were you born with it then?"

"I think I must have been," Thérèse said gravely.

Céline snorted and went out, closing the door with quite unnecessary vigour.

Left alone, Thérèse picked up her own disgraced dolls and put them back in their basket, arranging them conscientiously. She was always very careful with her family of wood and china babies, but she couldn't work up much affection for them. Their stiff legs and arms and vacant smiles irritated her. She much preferred the linnets and canaries which were kept in a big cage up in the attic room that Pauline had as her own private domain. Pauline needed a private place where she could meditate in preparation for the day when she would enter Carmel. Carmel was where the holy nuns lived, enclosed behind their grilles. Papa had told her about them and how they gave up the world in order to pray for souls. Thérèse thought it would be more exciting to be a martyr, burned at the stake like Joan of Arc, but Papa said that it was best to wait and see what God sent and not trouble Him too often. Thérèse had tried not to bother God too often, but there were times when she had so much to tell Him that the words bubbled out of her.

Now, her dolls put away, she opened the door and went down the stairs to the big kitchen where Pauline was baking. The scent of fresh bread filled her nostrils and a wire tray of cinnamon cakes attracted her eye. She stood as close as she could, her hands behind her back to keep them away from temptation.

Pauline, straightening up from her task, said without annoyance,

28

"Get your nose out of there, young lady. Céline is in the garden if you're looking for her."

"I don't wish to play with Céline," Thérèse said, removing her nose from the vicinity of the cakes and sticking it up in the air.

"You've not quarrelled?" Pauline asked.

"Not exactly quarrelled," Thérèse said, "but Céline hurt my feelings."

"You think too much about your own feelings," Pauline said, bringing another batch of cakes out of the oven. "You ought to think about others more."

"I do try," Thérèse said. "It's just that I'm always the youngest and the littlest. I'll never be able to catch the rest of you up, and I do try."

"It's no crime being the youngest and smallest," Pauline said briskly.

"Sometimes when I'm at Mass with you and Papa and the others," Thérèse confided, "I worry that even God might not notice me. If I'm such a little person then I must have a little soul, and He can't do much with that."

Pauline hesitated and then said, "Go and get the vase from the dining room, and the thimble from my sewing box, there's a good girl.'

Puzzled, Thérèse did as she was bade, setting the big glass vase and the tiny thimble side by side on the table.

"Now fill them with water from the jug. Right to the brim," Pauline ordered.

Kneeling upon the stool, Thérèse carefully poured the water in until it splashed over the top.

"Which one is the fuller?" Pauline enquired.

"They're both full," Thérèse said, squinting at them.

"Souls are like that," Pauline said. "Big ones and little ones are filled with grace to their brim, and each holds as much as it can contain, without envy of the other."

"You know everything, Pauline," Thérèse said wistfully.

"Not everything," Pauline said, whisking her small sister off the chair and putting a cinnamon bun in each hand. "One for you and one for Céline, and don't argue with her."

She watched the small figure trot out and turned back to her work with a sigh. Thérèse was growing up fast though she didn't realize it. In a year or so she would be ready for school and once she was settled there only a little time was left before Pauline herself would enter Carmel. It would be a wrench to leave home but there were often times when she longed for the quietness of a cell and only muted chanting to break the silence of her thoughts.

"I wanted all of you to enter the religious life," Zélie had confided in the early stages of her illness. "It was a terrible disappointment when I was refused admission, but God had other plans for me. He wanted me to raise children to His service, and I have never regretted bearing one of you, but you are all so pretty I fear you'll want to get married and have children yourselves."

"I shall enter Carmel," Pauline had said. "As soon as I am twenty-one, Mamma, and the little ones are at school, I'll apply for admission to the novitiate."

"Not just because I want it?" Zélie had questioned anxiously. "I wouldn't want to force any of you."

"No need to force me," Pauline had said steadily. "I have inherited your vocation, Mama, for I never wanted to do anything else."

She had been a schoolgirl then with her hair down her back and now she was a young woman, braids coiled around her head, but her determination had never wavered, only it would be hard to leave Thérèse who had become the nearest to a child of her own that she would ever know.

Thérèse had carried the cakes into the garden where

Céline was walking up and down, scuffing the gravel with her toe.

"I've brought you a cake from Pauline," she announced, handing over the fragrant bun.

"I'll play with you when I've eaten it," Céline said, her good humour restored. "You can be my darling daughter."

"I've thought of a new game," the other said. "Can we play that instead?"

"What sort of game?" Céline wanted to know. "If it's walking with your eyes shut, pretending to be blind, I don't think we'd better. The last time you and Cousin Marie played that game you knocked down a big pile of boxes outside a shop and the lady was very cross."

"It's a new game," Thérèse insisted. "It's called 'Hermits'. We pretend to be hermits, like the ancient desert fathers that Papa was reading us a story about."

"The ones who sat on pillars of stone?"

"They didn't all do that," Thérèse objected. "Sometimes they lived in pairs, and one went out into the fields to work and the other one stayed in the hut and prayed."

"What did they talk about?"

"They took vows of silence," Thérèse said gravely. "That saved them having to think up subjects for conversation. Do play, Céline. It's a beautiful game."

"Finish your cake then," Céline said.

Thérèse flung the remaining crumbs to a scatter of small birds on the lawn and stood, her arms folded, looking up at her sister.

"You can choose," she said generously, "whether to work or pray."

"I'll work," Céline said. "I always make the bed and hang up your clothes anyway."

"And I shall be like the Magdalen and pray," Thérèse said, going happily to her plot of garden where a new altar,

31

decorated with ivy, had been erected by her the previous day.

Pauline, coming out to call them for supper, found them in perfect amity, with Thérèse prostrate before her altar while Céline mowed an imaginary field a few yards away.

The little ones were allowed to stay up an extra half hour that night as Louis was going to Alençon on business for two or three days. His infrequent absences from home were greeted by Thérèse with floods of tears and only the prospect of an extra song or story consoled her for his departure.

When the meal had been cleared away the draught board was brought out and an extra lamp lit, so that Marie and Pauline could sew in comfort. Thérèse adored draughts, she and Céline taking on Papa jointly and collapsing in helpless giggles when he made mistakes that enabled them to win time after time.

"You are too clever for me," he said at last, throwing up his hands in mock despair. "I tell you, girls, you put me to shame with your skill."

"But we can't sing as well as you can," Thérèse said quickly. "Do sing something, Papa!"

"Shall I sing 'Bluebeard'?" he enquired, amused.

"Oh, no!" Céline shrieked. "Uncle Isidore sings that when we visit him on Sunday evenings, and it frightens us into fits! Sing something nicer."

"An Easter hymn," Thérèse begged. "I know it's not Easter yet, but I love the Festival so much."

"An Easter song then."

With the youngest girls perched on his knees and the eldest lowering their needlework in order to listen more intently, he let his fine tenor voice ring through the cosy parlour.

"Another, Papa!" Thérèse implored, but Pauline was

glancing towards the clock and shaking her head.

"Time for prayers." Louis, who never undermined the older girl's authority, put the children down and reached in his pocket for his rosary.

This was the moment of the day that Thérèse loved best. Kneeling at the end of the row, she stole glances from beneath her eyelashes at her father who knelt opposite to them, his long, sensitive jeweller's hands fingering each bead of his carved black rosary. The actual prayers bored her a little, for she could never concentrate on the meaning of them for more than a few seconds at a time, but she liked to hear his voice rolling out the words and the lighter tones of her sisters as they made their responses.

"Good-night, princess."

She must have dozed off for a few minutes for Papa was holding her up by the elbows and laughing.

"Good-night, Papa. Sleep well. Come home safe!" she shrilled flinging her arms about his neck and burrowing her face in his shoulder.

"Come, Thérèse." Pauline lifted her and bore her through the door and up the stairs.

Tucked in the big bed where Céline would join her an hour later, Thérèse caught at her sister's skirt.

"Couldn't you leave the lamp, just for a few minutes?" she pleaded.

"Big girls of seven can manage to get to sleep without lights," Pauline said firmly.

"It's so dark."

"Darkness never hurt anyone," Pauline reproved. "You've been a good girl today so you need have no fear. Why, there are angels thronging all around your bed, pet!"

She kissed Thérèse swiftly and went out, taking the lamp with her. Darkness shrouded the room, turning each piece of furniture into a lurking beast that crouched ready to spring at her as soon as she closed her eyes. She tried to imagine angels thronging round, their white wings feathering the air, their haloes hidden by the dark, but it was impossible to think of anything but the grotesque creatures waiting to spring upon her. Tears forced themselves between her lids and rolled down her cheeks, and she prayed silently for time to pass quickly so that Céline could join her and share the nameless terror that stalked the dark room.

Morning brought sunlight and the singing of birds. The night fears dissipated with the last trails of mist clinging to the treetops, and she stretched luxuriously in the warmth of the bed. Céline, who was a day pupil at the Benedictine Abbey, was already dressing, and Pauline was coming in with two mugs of hot chocolate.

"Papa went an hour since," she said cheerfully. "He left word that you were not to cry for him, Thérèse, because he will be back in two or three days and he'll bring a present for you."

It was impossible not to shed a few tears because the brightness of the morning was dimmed, but she wiped them away with the corner of the sheet and even achieved a shaky smile.

"You must work hard at your lessons," Pauline said, "and earn a big silver star to show Papa when he comes home."

That prospect cheered her immensely. She enjoyed her lessons with her sisters, particularly the history ones. And Pauline and Marie were always very fair when they marked her exercises, never giving her credit when she didn't deserve it. She resolved to work as hard as possible to make Papa proud of her when he returned.

Despite her good intentions she found that the hours dragged, with no walks in the afternoons and only Marie to lead the evening prayers. Céline's return from school each day was greeted with squeals of delight.

"You can feed my linnets if you like," Pauline said at last.

It was the third day of Louis's absence and Thérèse was visibly drooping. She had hung around Marie while Pauline was instructing Victoire in her duties, had built two altars and pulled them down, and was now swinging disconsolately on the newel post at the foot of the stairs.

Armed with bird seed Thérèse ran up to the attic and began her task, her face brightening as the linnets chirped at her. Some of them were trying to imitate the louder song of the canaries and she whistled back at them, her small fingers scrabbling through the bars. A ray of sunlight pierced the gloom and she went over to the window and looked down into the garden with its stone bench and the oval rose bed in the centre of the green lawn.

Louis was walking slowly across the lawn, his hands clasped behind his back. She wrenched open the casement and called down to him, but he went on walking at the same steady, unhurried pace. Despite the warmth of the sun on her neck and face, Thérèse felt suddenly cold as if darkness had come and brought back the lurking beasts. The figure looked and walked like Papa, but his head was swathed in a thick, greyish veil so that his features were obscured.

Terror suddenly swamping her, she gripped the sill, screaming out his name over and over, but as Marie and Pauline rushed in the figure was gone and the garden was warm again.

THREE

There were times when Thérèse wondered if schools had
been invented just to give children the opportunity of
suffering. She had been a day pupil at the Benedictine Abbey
for a year and hated it more every day.

The lessons were no problem. Thanks to Pauline's careful
training she was ahead of her age in most subjects and had
been placed in a class with bigger girls. As long as she lived
she would remember standing in the playground with a
circle of them around her, all firing questions so that she
became quite dizzy with trying to answer.

"Thérèse Martin. Alençon. My sisters and my Papa take
care of me. We have one servant, named Victoire—Yes,
Léonie is my sister but she's left school now. My big sister,
Marie, always curls my hair for me in this way. No, I
have no mother but my sister, Pauline, is my mother now."

They had crowded nearer and nearer until she had the
impression that they would squash her flat and had felt
herself shrinking smaller and smaller in the midst of them.
She had on her new blue dress with a yoke of white lace,
and her ringlets were tied in two bunches with ribbons
that matched her eyes.

"My princess will be the loveliest girl in the school,"
Louis had said fondly.

Thérèse wasn't at all sure that she wanted to be the
loveliest girl in the school. What she did want was to make
some friends who would play with her and with whom
she could exchange secrets.

36

"You're very small," one of the girls said critically. "Are you a dwarf?"

"No, indeed I'm not!" Her colour rose indignantly.

"You don't look more than five," another remarked.

"I'm eight and a half," she said trying to speak with dignity, but finding, with horror, her voice beginning to quiver ominously.

"She's going to cry," said a plump girl with her eyes narrowed and her head on one side as if Thérèse were some queer zoological specimen.

"I am not so!" But tears were already beading her lashes and she hung her head.

"What game would you like to play?"

"You can play with us if you like," said another in a kindly manner. "Would you like to play?"

"Yes, very much." Thérèse blinked furiously and lifted her head.

"What game do you like best?" someone asked.

"At home I play Hermits and Martyrs," she said.

"What a funny name for a game!" someone exclaimed. "How do you play it?"

"Well, those who are hermits go round and pick up the dead leaves, pretending they are herbs for the healing of the sick and then they kneel down and pray, and the ones who are martyrs pretend to be burned and beheaded. And some of us could be angels and fly about singing hymns to encourage the others," Thérèse said eagerly.

"I never heard of such a silly game in my life!" the plump damsel said scornfully. "Don't you like playing other games?"

"Oh, yes!" Thérèse plunged on, her little face earnest. "At home I play at Missionaries too. Some of us could be the missionaries and the others the poor pagan savages. I usually have my dolls for that, but we could have real

37

people for that here and it would be much more interesting."

"Wouldn't you like to play ball?" the kind-voiced girl asked.

"Oh, yes! I have a red ball at home and Céline and I roll it across the lawn and see if we can get it to roll into a little hole."

"We play Catch here. You stand in the middle and one of us throws the ball and you must jump up and catch it," the girl said.

The circle was widening and she was left standing in the middle. Something whizzed through the air above her head and then whizzed back again. She jumped with her arms upstretched, but the ball eluded her grasp and, in turning, she slipped and fell, not heavily but with such a lack of grace that several of them laughed.

"I don't want to play this game!" she gasped scrambling up. "I have a hoop. We could bowl a hoop."

"Bowling hoops is for babies," one of the girls said.

"That's what she is," said another. "Just a silly baby! Baby! Baby!"

A few of them took up the chorus and then a bell rang somewhere and the nun in charge came out to marshal them into line, favouring Thérèse with a hard stare as the latter came panting up. The new pupil, with her frilled dress and elaborately curled hair, was clearly a spoiled little madam. She hoped the child wouldn't display the same difficult temperament as he sister, Léonie.

Thérèse sometimes wondered if there was something wrong with her that the family didn't notice. After that first day she had tried hard to make friends, but none of the other girls wanted to play any of the games she invented, or to share secrets with her. At playtime they either teased her or ignored her. Céline was in another class and came out to play at a different time. In any event Céline had her own group of friends, and Thérèse knew that telling tales was a very wicked thing to do. Pauline had always impressed that upon her.

"If any of your schoolmates are rough or unkind you must smile and say nothing about it, and then they will respect you," Pauline had said.

Thérèse tried hard to obey, never saying anything about the sly pinches and shoves inflicted on her, but she found it impossible to smile very much. Most of the time she was either choking back tears or wiping away a fresh flood.

"I never saw such a cry baby," Father Domin said in exasperation, shaking his head over Thérèse who sat in the front row of the class, vigorously blowing her nose. "What ails you now? You only lost one mark in the test."

"I didn't know the name of the father of Moses," Thérèse sobbed.

She was not really crying about that at all, but about the fact that when she had offered to help one of the teachers put out the pencils the nun had snapped,

"You must learn not to try to curry favour!"

"You must try to control yourself," Father Domin said. "Now dry your eyes and pay attention to me. And do sit up straight! You're such a clever girl that it's a great pity you're so babyish!"

He hadn't meant to be unkind, but she had cried all over again when he said that, and when the playbell rang she had hurried away to the furthest corner of the grounds and sat down under a tree out of sight of the other girls.

There was a dead sparrow lying near her feet and she picked it up, holding it gently in her hands. It seemed a great pity that it should be here all by itself with nobody to mourn it. After a moment she scooped out a little hole with her fingers in the soft earth, laid the tiny corpse within, and smoothed the earth over it again. There were some daisies growing in a clump nearby and she picked some and stuck them in a pattern on the grave. The whole effect was very pleasing and she made the sign of the cross over it with great satisfaction. In future, when she could evade the other girls with their rough ways and their teasing, she would slip away here and play the new game of Funerals.

But school itself continued to be a penance. She dreaded the moment every morning when Pauline kissed her good-bye at the school gate and Céline and she walked up the curved path to the huge, gaunt building with its echoing corridors and its mingled smells of chalk, ink, and beeswax. Playtimes were the worst, for though her cemetery was coming along nicely it wasn't always possible to avoid the bigger girls who made her the butt of their jokes. She enjoyed her lessons, especially history, but when she tried to help her slower companions by whispering the right answers to them they called her a show off, and when she offered to help the teachers by cleaning the blackboard and putting out the exercise books she was told not to put herself forward.

The last bell of the day was her signal for release, and she flew down the path with her schoolbag bumping on her shoulder and her hat crammed down on top of her head. A whole wonderful evening ahead before family prayers and the darkness of the night!

Pauline was the model on which she tried to fashion herself. The memory of Zélie had somehow or other been combined in her mind with the present reality of her quiet elder sister, and there were times when she thought of Pauline as her real mother. Pauline was always so calm and strong, always ready to answer questions and give advice. It was Papa who devised little treats for his princess, taking her fishing with him on Sunday afternoons, giving her extra pocket money so that she could buy something nice for Céline, but Papa was sometimes melancholy and withdrawn or away on business. It was Pauline who was the anchor of her existence, and the day was not complete until Pauline had assured her she had been a good girl and deserved another jewel for her heavenly crown.

One afternoon, sitting on the garden bench, Thérèse was making a little straw basket with some lengths of coloured raffia that Léonie had given her. Léonie was at home now, and though she was much improved in temper she spent a lot of her time at her uncle's house. Uncle Isidore was particularly fond of Léonie, declaring that for all her clumsiness and lack of learning, she had in her the makings of a remarkable woman. Thérèse certainly hoped so, for she knew that Papa worried a great deal about his third daughter and had many Masses offered on her behalf. She bent her head over her work, carefully threading the raffia in and out. The basket was to be a present for Pauline's twenty-first birthday and Thérèse intended to fill it with flowers and tie one of her hair ribbons to the handle. Through the open window above her head the voices of her two elder sisters floated out into the sunny garden.

"It is not simply because Mamma wished it. I have never considered doing anything else but enter Carmel."

"It will be a wrench for us when you go," came Marie's quieter voice.

"You will be able to manage, won't you? Victoire is fully trained and Léonie is very much better these days."

"Oh, I shall manage beautifully! It is not as if you are going far away from us. We will be able to visit you in the parlour on Thursdays."

41

The raffia had fallen unheeded to the ground and Thérèse was on her feet, running round to the door.

"Pauline! Pauline, you're not going away, are you?" she gasped, bursting into the room where her sisters were chatting.

"Only to Carmel," Pauline said, calmly laying aside her knitting.

"You can't! You can't!" Thérèse cried.

"You always knew that I would enter Carmel one day, pet," Pauline began, but Thérèse interrupted her, beginning to sob.

"Yes, but not yet! Not yet! You said you were going when you were grown up! And you promised that I could come with you!"

"Sweetheart, that was just a joke. You were never meant to take it seriously!" Pauline exclaimed.

"But you said it. You said it," Thérèse insisted, the tears now spurting in earnest. "When I said that I wished we could go and live on a desert island together and be hermits, you said that we would have to wait until I was a big girl. You promised!"

"It was a joke," Pauline repeated helplessly.

"But we need you here," Thérèse said. "You said you'd be my mamma when Mamma died! You can't be my mamma if you're locked up in Carmel!"

"We are not locked up. It is we who lock out the world."

"You want to lock me out? I thought you loved me dearly and that I was a good girl! It'll be Christmas soon and you know how you love Christmas with our presents in the shoes by the fireside and the big cake and the carol singing!"

"They have Christmas at Carmel too," Pauline said, smiling.

"It won't be the same," Thérèse said dolefully. "It won't

42

be like a real Christmas if you're not there. Papa won't let you go. I'll make him not let you!"

"Papa has known for years that I intended to enter the religious life one day. You knew it too."

"I forget about it," Thérèse said, and began to cry more violently, rocking herself to and fro.

"Darling, you must hush!" Pauline swiftly picked her up and sat down again with the child in her lap. "What will Papa say if he comes home and finds you in this state?"

"He will say you ought to stay at home so that I won't be in such a state!" Thérèse said promptly.

Pauline and Marie exchanged glances of wry amusement. Then Pauline hugged the small girl tightly even as she said placidly,

"Now listen to me, love. You're a big girl now, nearly ten years old, and far too sensible and good to behave like a baby. I promised God a long time ago that as soon as I was of age I would enter His service as a Sister of Carmel. Now would you want me to go back on my promise to God simply because you are upset about it? There's no merit in either of us then."

"If you are going to Carmel," Thérèse said, fiercely scrubbing at her eyes, "then I shall go with you."

"The life at Carmel," Pauline said, "is not a holiday but a vocation. Perhaps I ought to have talked more with you about it but in a way I feared to talk about it too much lest something happen that made it impossible for me to enter."

"Did you want to go so badly, to leave us all behind?" Thérèse's sobs were dwindling but her tears still flowed.

"It is not a case of 'wanting', Thérèse," Pauline said hesitatingly. "Carmel is the place chosen for me. That is what I mean by a vocation."

"Then I have a vocation too," Thérèse sat up and blew her nose on the handkerchief that Pauline gave her. "If Carmel is the place for you then it's my place too."

"Thérèse, that's silly!" Marie began, but Pauline said,

"Perhaps you're right, sweetheart, God may have chosen Carmel as your place too. We shall have to wait and see."

Thérèse said nothing, but her expression was brooding. It was, of course, impossible for Pauline to leave her. On the other hand it was impossible for Pauline to break the promise she had made to God. So they would have to go together. For a moment her head quailed at the thought of leaving Papa and her sisters, but Pauline came first. To lose Pauline would be like lifting her eyes to see Zélie's coffin again.

"What will Pauline do all the time she is in Carmel?" she enquired of Marie later.

"Pray and make sacrifices," Marie said curtly. "The nuns give up all their pleasures and lock themselves away from the world in order to pray for the world."

It sounded to Thérèse like a splendid way of passing one's life. Marie, however, was untangling the knots in her small sister's curls and something in her face warned the child to drop the subject.

She took it up again with Pauline as soon as the two had a few minutes alone together.

"When you go into Carmel, won't you be my sister-mother any more?"

"I shall always be that," Pauline said gently, "but the other nuns will be my sisters too, and it will be my duty to love them equally."

"I wish one could see Carmelites," Thérèse said, slanting a glance at the older girl. "I've only ever heard them singing behind the big grille in church."

"Would you like to come with me to the parlour on

44

Sunday when I go to see Mother Prioress?" Pauline enquired.

"Could I? Could I tell her that I'm going to be a Carmelite too?"

"If you like," Pauline said, indulgently. "She'll be very interested, I'm sure."

"Pauline, you're the best sister that ever lived!" Thérèse cried, flinging her arms about her.

"Careful or you'll have me off balance!" Pauline disengaged herself, thinking with a little pang that very soon even the most innocent caresses would be forbidden to her.

Sunday came round more slowly than a birthday. Thérèse found it almost impossible to contain her excitement, and could have wept with impatience when Pauline stopped to exchange a few words with some neighbours on their way to church.

She had often seen the high walls of the convent with its connecting passage to the church, but she had never before climbed the stone steps to a bare room with nothing in it save a few chairs and a crucifix on the wall. It was quite unlike any parlour she had ever seen.

"Sit down, there's a good girl." Pauline pressed her down to a chair, patted her shoulder and went out.

In front of Thérèse, a shutter was rolled back, revealing a mesh grille behind which a tall nun with a proud, hawk face stood, her hands hidden in her wide sleeves.

"I am Mother Marie Gonsague," she said, bowing slightly.

Thérèse was not certain if it was correct to curtsey, so she bowed her head as politely as she could and said,

"I am Marie-Françoise Thérèse Martin."

"Pauline's little sister, Thérèse. She has spoken of you to me often."

The Prioress sat down on a stool behind the grille and fixed dark, intelligent eyes on her small visitor.

"I wanted to see you," Thérèse said.

"And how may I help you?" the Prioress enquired.

Thérèse hesitated. Usually she was tongue-tied in the presence of strangers but something in the other's calm enquiring gaze brought the words flowing out.

"I have a vocation for the religious life, Mother Prioress. I am anxious to do God's Will and enter Carmel at once, if you will accept me."

"You know that your sister, Pauline, will be joining us very soon?"

"Yes, I do, but I have a vocation quite on my own account," Thérèse said earnestly.

"I am certain you have," the Prioress said without smiling. "There is only one thing that prevents me from admitting you at once."

"I do try very hard to be good," Thérèse said.

"It isn't that, child. It's your age."

"I shall be ten on the second of January," Thérèse said quickly. "I know I look younger because I'm not very tall, but I'm nearly always top of my class."

"We don't accept postulants until they are sixteen," the Prioress said.

"Sixteen!" Thérèse's mouth fell open in dismay. "But that's six years away—more than half the years I've lived already!"

"One moment, please." The Prioress raised her hand and inclined her head as another Sister came into view behind the grille.

"Mother Prioress, you asked me to join you in the parlour?" the newcomer said.

"Indeed I did. I wished you to meet your little namesake, Thérèse Martin. Thérèse, this is Sister Teresa of St Augustine."

"What a pretty little girl!" the nun exclaimed, clasping

46

her hands. "How old is she?"

"Ten on January the second," Thérèse said, wishing that Sister Teresa hadn't mentioned her looks.

"She is a dear little thing," the other persisted. "Have you decided what to do when you grow up, Thérèse?"

"She hopes to join us in Carmel," the Prioress said. "I have just been explaining that we accept girls as postulants when they are sixteen."

"Oh, by then such a pretty girl will have a handsome beau," Sister Teresa said. "She'll not want to lock herself away from the world and hide that lovely face!"

Thérèse wished it were permissible to tell a holy nun not to be so silly. The interview was spoiled and Mother Prioress was already rising to leave.

"I really do want to enter the religious life," she said a little desperately.

"And you must keep that resolve bright and shining," the Prioress said kindly. "God bless you, child."

The shutters were being rolled back again and she was alone in the bare parlour with the crucifix on the wall. Sixteen! It was years and years away. Disappointed tears filled her eyes and fell down her cheeks. Aloud she said, "I do want to be a Carmelite! Truly I do. Not just because of Pauline but because this is the place chosen for me. I know it."

She looked sadly round the white-washed room, her tears still streaking her face. There was something here that caught her imagination and her heart, some indefinable essence that was unlike anything she had ever known. It seemed so cruel that she must be sixteen before she could enter the enchanted world beyond the shutters.

"I am to be Sister Agnes of Jesus," Pauline told her as they walked home together. "That will be my new name in religion. The Sisters get together and choose a name for the new postulant, and they chose Agnes for me. I was so pleased with their choice for I've always had a great devotion to the little martyr of Rome."

So there would be no more Pauline. There would only be Sister Agnes of Jesus who could be seen on Thursdays behind the grille, and it would be six years before she could join her. Anything might happen in six years! She herself might die or fall ill. She wondered if Pauline would be permitted to come home if she fell ill, so ill that she was almost dying.

"So you must be a good, brave girl," Pauline was saying. "You must help Marie all you can for I'm sure she will feel lonely when I'm gone."

Thérèse supposed that was true, but she couldn't imagine anyone feeling as bereft as she would be when Pauline became Sister Agnes.

FOUR

"You must be very proud to have a big sister in Carmel," Father Domin said.

His eyes, resting on the small figure before him, were anxious. Thérèse Martin was one of his brightest pupils, showing a grasp of religious matters far beyond her years, but she was painfully sensitive, finding it impossible to make friends of her classmates. Much of her time was spent in tears and, when she had been consoled, she cried all over again for having been so foolish as to get upset in the first place.

"Yes, Father," she whispered. "Pauline is Sister Agnes of Jesus now."

"And your other sisters are well?"

"Yes, thank you, Father."

"And you, Thérèse? You look a little pale."

"I have a headache," she murmured.

"Thérèse always has a headache these days," the nun in charge said in an aside. "Too highly strung for her own good."

"Perhaps the fresh air will do her good. Run along now, Thérèse, and enjoy your Easter holidays," Father Domin said heartily.

Thérèse went out sedately. She would have liked to run, but every step she took sent needles of pain shooting through her head. In the six months since Pauline had left the headaches had become more frequent and her nights were hideous with dreams that spilled over into waking life, so that cracks in a wall turned into gloating faces and flower heads crawled with worms.

She and Céline were spending the holiday with Uncle Isidore and Aunt Elisa, Louis having taken Marie and Léonie to spend a few days in Paris.

"We are going to give you a perfectly splendid time!" Uncle Isidore had declared. "The weather is so mild that we will be able to have picnics and go for drives into the country, and there are several social evenings you will enjoy."

Thérèse was not sure that she would. Her head hurt so much when she tried to move quickly and sometimes she had the unpleasant impression that a sheet of glass separated her from the rest of the world. Even parts of her own body seemed to her to be unreal as if they belonged to somebody else.

It was impossible to begin to explain how she felt because she couldn't explain it properly even to herself. There were days when she felt perfectly well, and then the heavy cloud would descend over her again, and hours would pass without her being fully aware of what had happened. She had never felt so completely alone. When they visited Pauline in the parlour at Carmel, they saw her only behind a grille, speaking mainly to the elders and giving Thérèse only a fleeting smile as they rose to go. Marie was always busy with the duties of the household, or with keeping Léonie company. Even Céline, at fourteen, was changing, her childish figure rounding out, her eyes full of secrets that Thérèse couldn't share.

Her headache had faded by the time she reached her uncle's house and she paused thankfully to savour the moments without pain, but when she went upstairs to take off her jacket and hat her legs began to shake so much that she had to cling to the banisters to keep herself upright.

"Something is troubling you," Uncle Isidore said abruptly, looking up from his newspaper as his niece paused on the threshold of his study.

"I was thinking about Pauline," she said, twisting the ends of her sash in her fingers.

"She will be received into the novitiate very soon. That will be a great day for us," he said.

"She will be the 'bride of Christ'," Thérèse said.

"An honour for the whole family to give a daughter to God," he nodded.

"Oh, it's not like that!" Her little face flushed as she tried to explain her meaning. "It is God who chooses us, and we must obey or be found wanting. But we have to prepare for the day when He does choose. We have to trim the wicks of our lamps and prime them with oil."

"And have you primed your lamp?" he asked tolerantly.

"Oh, yes!" She brought a small notebook out of her pocket and read from it. "Eight hundred and eighteen sacrifices and two thousand, seven hundred and seventy three acts of love in the past three months. My faults are in the other column, two hundred and——"

"My dear child!" Isidore Guérin looked up at her with anxiety.

"It's to help me keep count," she said earnestly. "It's not to be vain or boastful, truly!"

"Sweetheart, you're too serious for your years," he said. "Little girls shouldn't think so deeply about such matters."

"God might take us at any time to render up account."

"That's true, but you are such a good child——"

"Then my sacrifices will do to help other people," she said eagerly.

"I would like to hear less of sacrifice and more of fun and merriment," her uncle said. "Your Mamma—my sister, God rest her soul! used to laugh so much about the comical things you did when you were a tot! She used to call you her little imp."

"Mamma went to Heaven," Thérèse said. "She wanted to be a nun, but God called her to marriage instead because he wished her to have a family of saints. Papa told me."

"Your father is undoubtedly a saint," Isidore said wryly, "but he didn't realize that he had such a receptive audience in his youngest daughter! Now, put that book away, my love. We are going out to a Social Evening later, with games and dancing. Your Mamma used to enjoy such occasions."

But Mamma was a waxen yellow doll in a box and Pauline was locked up behind a grille. Thérèse looked down at her hands and saw that they were shaking as much as her legs. She tried to answer her uncle, but her teeth were clenched together, and the sheet of glass was all about her again.

Life was fragmented like the little pieces of coloured paper in the bottom of her kaleidoscope. Her uncle was there, looming over her with a smile on his face that terrified her as much as when he had sung 'Bluebeard'. Then his place was taken by Aunt Elisa whose plump face was crumpled with worry as she piled blankets about her niece. Céline's voice rose up in a cacophony of other sounds.

"What's wrong with Thérèse? Why isn't she coming with us?"

"Thérèse isn't very well, my dear. She is going to have an early night."

A gap, a space of nothingness, and then the doctor's big hand holding her wrist, his voice somewhere above her head.

"I've never seen anything like this before in so young a child. One might diagnose it as St Vitus Dance but that there are several features missing."

"Ought my brother-in-law to be recalled from Paris?"

"No need to alarm him yet. Keep her warm and quiet and we'll see how she goes on."

She wanted Papa and Marie very badly, but it was useless to call for them. When she tried their names came out all wrong and if they walked into the bedroom now they would see all her sins written up on the wall. Once when her father had called her she had answered, "Come here yourself!" That was a terrible thing to say to a father. A lady had looked at her when she was in the park and exclaimed to Papa, "What a beautiful little girl you have." And she had been pleased to hear herself admired.

"Did Pauline go into Carmel because I was such a bad girl?"

"No, of course not! You've always been a very good girl."

"I must go and see Pauline when she takes the veil."

"If you're feeling well enough then you may certainly go."

Pauline would wear a white dress with flowers in her hair, and her bridegroom would be Christ himself.

Papa had returned, or perhaps had been there for a day or two. Her sense of time was all muddled up.

"Oh, Papa, look what Pauline has sent me!"

A little wooden doll in the habit of a Carmelite lay in the box.

"I would like to hear rather less about Carmel in this house," Uncle Isidore said slowly.

But the little doll was like a promise. The cloud of fear and unreality was lifting and she felt hungry.

"As soon as the ceremony is over it's back to Les Buissonets and straight to bed!"

"I'll do anything you say, Marie, but do let me see Pauline at her Clothing!"

It was a glorious spring day and they all had on their best clothes. Marie had curled her hair and there were cornflowers on her new straw hat. Thérèse's eyes shone bluer than the cornflowers as she watched Pauline enter the church, with the train of her white dress foaming into ruffles of lace and Papa so distinguished in his frockcoat, leading her to the altar. Pauline looked quietly contented, as if she were doing exactly what she had always wanted to do. It would be selfish to wish her back.

She was no longer Pauline now but Sister Agnes of Jesus. As if Marie had gleaned the thought she bent to whisper to Thérèse. "I will be your mamma now, sweetheart."

So she was not really losing anything at all. Thérèse squeezed her sister's hand and beamed, craning her neck to see the glittering altar with its candles flaming.

They drove back to Buissonets, chattering and laughing, with the glory of the ceremony and the spring day all about them.

It was good to be home again. Thérèse dashed out into the garden to see if any of her flowers were out. She had dug them up so often to inspect the roots that Papa had declared it would be a miracle if any of them survived, but there were daffodils and a crocus nodding at her from the soil, and when she ran up to the attic her linnets and canaries chirped and whistled as if they knew exactly who she was and where she had been.

Thérèse chirped back at them and laughed. The attic rang with the whistling of the birds and her own shrill laughter. On and on and on. World without end. The devil sets traps for the unwary, waiting to drag bad children to hell. She was dancing to keep the devil away, somersaulting and cart-wheeling, flinging out her arms and legs in all directions. There were running footsteps on the stairs and Marie, or perhaps it was the devil, rushed in and began to call for Papa.

Thérèse had split into two. One part of her knew that it was all pretending, a ruse to make Pauline stop being Sister Agnes and come home again. The other part of her shrieked and moaned, leaping in and out of bed, grimacing, counting her sins over and over again.

"The case is beyond my skill," Dr Notta said. "If she were fourteen or fifteen I would suspect hysteria due to delayed menstruation, but not at ten years old. I would advise you to call in a specialist in mental disease."

So they thought she was going mad, did they? No doubt that was why they were trying to poison her, pretending that it was medicine. She closed her mouth firmly, her eyes staring past them to where pictures hung on charred fingers growing out of the wall. If she was very clever she could leave her body and it wouldn't matter what they did to it then. It lay there on the bed with its eyes closed, arms and legs limp as a rag doll, and Thérèse grinned down from the ceiling.

She was in Marie's bed, and there was a statue of the Blessed Virgin at the side of the bed. Lucky Marie to have such a pretty statue.

"Anything that will benefit the child, Louis! You have only to name it," Isidore Guérin said.

"Not so many people are so blessed in their relatives as we are in you," Louis said gratefully.

"As soon as she is well you must all go for a holiday at the seaside. Trouville now—she would like Trouville."

"If she ever gets well," Louis said heavily. "The specialist fears there will be permanent mental derangement, but I cannot accept such a verdict. She was always such a sensible little girl. Now if it had been Léonie——"

"Léonie is growing into a fine young woman," Isidore interrupted.

55

"Yes, but she has had her difficulties. I might have understood it if Léonie had had such an illness, but not Thérèse. God knows, but since poor Zélie was taken I have protected my little sweetheart from any evil that might befall her."

"You are the world's best father," Isidore agreed.

"I would lay down my life for any of my daughters," Louis said, "and they know it. And yet when I went in to see my little Thérèse, she screamed out that I was a great black beast, crushing the life out of her. It must have been the devil himself who put such words into her mouth!"

"Don't allow yourself to dwell on it," Isidore advised.

"But it's over a month since the attacks started again," Louis said. "It is wearing us all out. She will only be quiet when Marie is with her, and poor Marie must have her meals and some sleep!"

"Elisa will come round and take over for a few hours," Isidore promised.

"I have sent to Notre Dame in Paris to ask for Masses for her recovery," Louis said. "Our Lady of Victories must take pity on her."

"Anything you want, you have only need to ask," Isidore repeated, feeling helpless in the face of such distress.

In Marie's room Léonie sat by the bed, trying to follow the story she was reading and keep an eye on Thérèse who tossed and turned, her eyes wild, her hands plucking the sheets. Only the previous day she had flung herself on the floor, banging her head against the wall and laughing and shouting.

"Sponge her with warm, salty water," the doctor had ordered.

Easier said than done! Thérèse had screeched like a banshee, crying out they were trying to drown her. In the end they had to give up the attempt and now she lay, eyes fixed on something only she could see, her small frame shaken by convulsive trembling.

"Mamma? Mamma? Mamma!" The voice rose higher and higher.

Léonie clapped her hands over her ears and hunched more closely over her book, trying to follow the words. Her reading was slow at the best of times, but it was impossible to concentrate with that voice going on and on.

"I was in the garden, pet, gathering some flowers," Marie said, hurrying into the room with a great bunch of marguerites in her hands. "Wouldn't you like to make a pretty wreath for the statue?"

The part of Thérèse that had never lost count of time watched the flowers with pleasure. They looked so pretty as Marie had said. Marie was pretty too, her fair hair braided but with tiny curls softening her brow and wreathing her ears. Vanity, vanity, all is vanity!

It was a stranger who was putting the flowers into the vase. The Thérèse who lay on the bed opened her mouth to scream.

"Sweetheart, it's only me! It's Marie, your little Mamma!"

But that was a lie. Mamma was turned into wax and put into the ground for flowers to grow. Mamma had been taken away from them and turned into Sister Agnes of Jesus. It wasn't fair to leave Papa. Dear kind Papa who never let the wind blow on his princess. Papa, the black beast, who wanted to kill his princess and put her in the ground for flowers to grow.

Marie and Léonie—or perhaps it was two devils—were on their knees, praying to the statue. Useless to pray to wood or wax. Useless to pray to anything because the black beast was waiting to muffle his head in a thick, grey veil and pace the garden, ready to jump out at his princess and strangle her.

"Mother of God, don't let me go out of my mind!" The cry was a silent one as the two halves of Thérèse fused into a whole.

The statue wasn't made of wood after all. It was made of blood and bone and flesh, clothed all with silver. A living woman stood there, smiling at the little figure in the bed. The little figure was herself, Thérèse Martin, and the woman was all the mothers that had ever been, radiant and loving, smiling without words while the light shimmered golden, enfolding them both.

"Is she dying?" Léonie asked, nervously plucking at Marie's sleeve.

"I want you to run downstairs and make a big bowl of hot soup," Marie said briskly. "Go on now, there's a good girl. Everything is going to be all right."

Thérèse felt weak but clear headed. Léonie was hurrying away and Marie was plumping up the pillows.

"Do you know who I am now?" she asked.

"Yes, of course." Thérèse blinked to bring her into focus again, for the brightness had faded and everything was ordinary.

"What did you see just now? I know you saw something," Marie said.

She didn't want to say. It had been a private moment, meant just for her and not for anyone else, but Marie looked so weary with all the night watching she had endured.

"It's a secret. You'll not tell?"

"Cross my heart," Marie promised.

"I saw the statue smile at me," Thérèse confided. "It wasn't a statue then but a real person, Marie. It was Our Lady. She smiled and all the bits of me flew together again."

"We must tell Pauline—Sister Agnes!" Marie exclaimed.

"No, no, it's a secret," Thérèse said in alarm. "I don't want anyone to know, not Papa, or Léonie, or anyone!"

"But Pauline has a right to know," Marie coaxed. "She's worn out her knees praying for your recovery, pet, and she's locked away in Carmel. Oh, but you must let me tell her. It'll be a secret still, but she has a right to know!"

Thérèse hesitated, then nodded reluctantly. No doubt Marie was right. Pauline ought to be told about the wonderful things that had happened.

"A slight muscular weakness but that will pass off," Dr Notta said, dropping Thérèse's wrist and smiling down at her. "You gave us all a very bad fright, young lady. You can get up tomorrow and go into the garden, get some colour back into those cheeks!"

"You don't anticipate a relapse?" Louis murmured, following him out of the room.

"She seems to me to be completely cured," the other told him. "To be perfectly honest with you, I'm still not certain of the nature of the ailment. In all my experience I've never come across anything quite like it before. She must be kept quiet, away from sudden shocks or excitements, and I would recommend a change of air as soon as she is strong enough to travel."

"I had planned to take the girls on a holiday if we were granted the favour of a cure," Louis began.

"Excellent! The seaside perhaps? Children love romping about on the beach."

"I considered that, but it seems to me that a quieter holiday would be more beneficial," Louis said. "August is the tenth anniversary of my dear wife's death, and it's been my wish to make a pilgrimage to her grave. That will please my little Thérèse."

"You know your daughter best, Monsieur Martin."

"I used to think so," said Louis sadly, "but there have

59

been times recently when I've felt as if I never really knew her at all. What caused her illness, Doctor? Was it some error on my part in the way I reared her? That thought has tormented me."

"If I were you I'd simply be thankful of her cure and not go looking for causes," Dr Notta said, shaking hands firmly, and smiling reassuringly.

"We must take good care of you," Marie said, curling Thérèse's hair and twining white ribbons through the ringlets. "Pauline—Sister Agnes, I mean, is so looking forward to seeing you again in the parlour! She won't believe that you're really well until she sees you with her own eyes!"

"I feel fine," Thérèse said, jumping up and hugging the other girl. "I feel like a chick bursting out of the shell!"

"Then stop flapping and let me put your jacket on," Marie said, laughing as her sister bounced up and down.

They walked to the Carmel, with Thérèse tugging at Marie's hand in her eagerness to be there quickly. It seemed years since she had been to the parlour, and Pauline must have been so anxious during her illness, dependent on what others related to her and not able to see for herself.

Going into the bare little parlour was like coming home. Thérèse wanted to sing and hum and dance with the sheer joy of reunion as she ran up to the grille. Mother Prioress was there, with Pauline and several of the other nuns. It was so good to see them again as they crowded to the mesh.

"Dear little Thérèse! Dear little girl! You look as if you had never been ill at all. It's by the mercy of Heaven that you were spared to us. To see the Blessed Virgin was a very great blessing!"

Kind faces and excited voices struck her like a blow. She looked reproachfully at Pauline.

"I had to tell them," Pauline said. "It would have been

very wrong to keep the news of a miracle to myself."

"Marie promised——" Thérèse began.

"I know, love, and we won't worry Papa or Léonie with it," Pauline said, "but these Sisters have a right to hear about it, for now they are my Sisters too, you know."

"Did you truly see Our Blessed Lady?" Mother Prioress asked.

"It was the statue, just in the beginning," Thérèse said. "Then it was a living lady. She smiled at me."

"Did she have the baby Jesus in her arms?"

"Was there a blaze of light about her head?"

"What did Our Lady say to you?"

Questions flew at her, and each one was like a tiny barb sticking into her mind.

"She just smiled at me," she repeated.

"And nothing else happened?"

"She just smiled," Thérèse said helplessly. "She just smiled at me, and she was so beautiful that I felt better, like a whole person again."

"But she must have said something! Are you, perhaps, not allowed to tell us?"

"At Lourdes the Soubirous child was given certain secrets which she has always refused to reveal."

"Was it perhaps something like that, dear?"

"She never said anything at all," Thérèse said. "She just smiled and I got better."

She could tell from their faces that they had expected more. If only she had followed her instincts and not told Marie in the first place none of this would have happened.

"Perhaps it was just a dream," one of the nuns said.

"Oh, no! It really happened!" Thérèse cried. "Really it did!"

But doubts were crowding into her mind. She had been ill, after all, and had seen some very strange things that

61

hadn't really been there at all. Perhaps the smiling statue had been part of the illness too, and it hadn't really happened.

"The main thing is that you are well again," Pauline said. "We have offered so many prayers for you, sweetheart."

But perhaps she hadn't really been ill. Perhaps the illness had only been in her own head.

"She is not to return to school until October," Marie said. "Papa has decided that she must be cherished at home for a few months until she is strong enough to face the world again, but we are going to Alençon in August."

"To see Mamma's grave? Oh, that will be a treat for you," Pauline cried.

"And if you do remember anything else about Our Lady's appearance you will come and tell us?" Mother Prioress asked.

"There wasn't anything. She just smiled at me," Thérèse said.

She felt utterly miserable. It had been a terrible mistake to confide in anyone, as if she had exposed some delicate flower to the air and it had immediately lost all its fragrance.

"This is her first trip out," Marie was saying. "You will forgive me if we don't stay too long?"

"Of course, you must hurry back before the air turns chill." Mother Prioress was rising, her hands folded within her wide sleeves. "God bless you, child. Never forget that you have been granted a great privilege."

"Mother Prioress." Thérèse dipped into her little curtsey. "Sister Agnes."

Not Pauline. Pauline was finally gone for ever as surely as if she had died, and Sister Agnes of Jesus stood behind the grille, with the calm, quiet dignity of a nun. Thérèse wished she could remember how the Blessed Virgin had smiled but the picture of it was growing as faint in her mind as the picture of Pauline with her braids swinging loose and a new dress on.

FIVE

The months leading up to Thérèse's first Holy Communion seemed to her to be interminable. To go up to the altar rail and kneel there to receive the sacred wafer of un-leavened bread under which the reality of the Godhead lay concealed had always been in her mind the most exciting mysterious action that any human could perform and even when she was tiny she had envied her older sisters the privilege for which she was too young. When they had gone off to Mass, she had persuaded Victoire to give her two little stubs of used candle to set up at each side of her toy altar and a bit of bread over which she made the sign of the cross with great fervour. Later when she had begun to go to church herself, she had longed with every fibre of her being to go up for Communion on the occasions when they went.

"I'm so little that I could slip in between you and pop up at the last minute, then the priest might give me the blessed bread before he thought about it," she had pleaded.

Pauline and Marie had scolded her for being silly. Good things were worth a little patience, Marie had said, and the days when even tiny babies were given Holy Com-munion had long since passed.

"At that time the Roman Emperors were persecuting the Christians," Marie explained, "so it was considered that even small children should be granted the right to receive Communion, for they might very well be called upon to be martyrs."

Martyrs went straight to Heaven, Thérèse knew, and she regretted very much that such an opportunity was unlikely to come her way. Yet one martyrdom didn't seem sufficient to merit an eternity of happiness. Thérèse thought she would not be content until she had suffered every kind of martyrdom. To be roasted on a gridiron, beheaded, burned at the stake, flayed, thrown to wild beasts, excited her imagination. Sacrifice! The very word had a glamour about it and she often went off to sleep at night picturing herself in scenes of unimaginable heroism. With steady fingers she combed her hair and walked out with the saints Perpetua and Felicity to face the savage bulls. With Joan of Arc she kissed the cross fashioned by a soldier and stood bound to the stake. With St Laurence she lay on a red hot gridiron, smiling through her agony.

In reality she found it a great nuisance even to make the bed when Céline was busy doing some other task. She did so occasionally and was bitterly hurt when Céline didn't notice or thank her. Although the strange illness of the previous year had not recurred she still spent much of her time in tears.

"If you waste all your tears now," Marie said in exasperation, "you'll have none left for your old age! I never, in all my days, knew anybody who could turn on the waterworks as thoroughly as you do!"

That had brought a fresh burst of weeping. Nobody, Thérèse thought miserably, understood her, but it wasn't really surprising when she found it impossible to understand herself.

Holy Communion would work a miraculous change in her. The silly weakness that made her dissolve into tears even at a look would be eradicated by the grace flooding into her soul. She would no longer mind that the other girls at school jeered at her long ringlets and pale, frilled

c

dresses, or that the teachers called her 'Cry-baby', and tried to shame her out of her fits of crying. She would be as brave and strong as the ancient martyrs.

What troubled her greatly was the delay before her ambition could be fulfilled. If she had been born just two weeks earlier she would have been allowed to make her first Communion six months before, but as it was she had to wait until the Easter after her eleventh birthday.

Seeing the bishop striding ahead of her as they walked back from Carmel one afternoon, she begged her sisters to let her run ahead and catch him up.

"I'll ask him if I can make my first Communion early as a special favour. Oh, do let me try!"

"You'll do no such thing," Léonie scolded, taking a firm grasp of her sister's belt. "His Lordship hasn't time for little girls who demand special treatment because they think that they're better than anybody else!"

"I don't think that!" Thérèse said indignantly. "I was born too late, that's my trouble."

"You were born when God willed it," Marie said in the flat tone which put an end to an argument. "Now stop being a nuisance."

"A pleasure deferred is a pleasure doubled," Céline said from the lofty heights of her fourteen years.

"I might not live to be *able* to make my first Communion," Thérèse said pathetically. "I might be murdered, like those people that Pranzini killed when he was doing that robbery."

"You're not supposed to know anything about that," Marie frowned. "Papa doesn't allow you to read newspapers."

"I don't read them, but it was written up in big letters on all the placards," she protested. "Pranzini is an unregenerate criminal who has refused all religious consola-

66

tion. The placards said so."

"Then you'd be better employed in praying for his conversion instead of bothering the bishop," Léonie said, winking at Marie.

The carefully tossed seed had taken root.

"Let's make a novena for the conversion of Pranzini," Thérèse suggested to Céline when they were alone.

"I don't think it would do much good," Céline said doubtfully. "He won't see a priest or confess or anything. I heard Papa telling Uncle Isidore that he was afraid that such a man would go straight to hell the minute he died."

"We could try," Thérèse said eagerly. "Oh, do let's try, Céline. We could use our pocket money and ask for a Mass for his repentance, and we could get up half an hour earlier every morning for nine days and pray for him. Oh, couldn't we do that?"

"If you want it," Céline said indulgently. She generally gave in to Thérèse's whims and this one seemed harmless.

"But you won't go upsetting yourself if he dies without repenting?" she cautioned.

"He will repent," Thérèse said calmly. "Even if we never hear anything about it I know that he will repent, but I shall pray for a sign too, some proof just for our own satisfaction. We'll get that sign. I just know we will!"

"You're always very sure of God," Céline disapproved.

"Because He is the only sure thing we have," Thérèse said simply.

The only sure thing in a shifting world. She clung to that thought in the dark nights after she had been put to bed and the lamp taken away. In the parlour downstairs there was still light and laughter, with Papa and Céline playing draughts together while Marie and Léonie sat and sewed. Upstairs she closed her eyes tightly against the threatening shadows and imagined herself in Carmel.

Nobody seemed to take her profession seriously. Even Pauline who was now Sister Agnes of Jesus had given her a faintly questioning glance on her last visit to Carmel and said, "You're certain it's not for my sake that you want to become a Carmelite?"

Perhaps that had been the start of it all, or perhaps it had begun in the hall at Alençon when she had seen her mother's coffin propped up against the wall and realized the meaning of separation, but she knew that even if her sister had remained in the world she would still have wanted to be a nun.

"I have written to Father Pichon, the chaplain of Carmel, and told him that I will be entering as soon as I possibly can," she confided to Marie.

"Thérèse, you had no right to do such a thing!" Marie exclaimed. "You must learn not to put yourself forward in such a manner!"

"But he will be my spiritual director when I take the veil," Thérèse said.

"Not another word!" Marie scolded her. "You must get this nonsense right out of your head. One of us in Carmel, is quite sufficient."

Thérèse held her peace. She would have liked to explain that she really wanted to be a saint, and becoming a nun was only the first step on a long road, but she was afraid that Marie would scold her even more fiercely if she ventured to say such an arrogant thing.

"I have been thinking that Céline ought to have lessons in drawing and painting," Louis said, coming into the parlour. "She has a real knack for catching a likeness."

"That's a splendid idea," Marie said warmly.

Thérèse clasped her hands together tightly. Drawing and painting were two activities that she had always loved, but art lessons were expensive.

"How about you, princess?" Louis enquired, turning towards her. "Would you like to learn to draw and paint too?"

"Thérèse has no aptitude," Marie said irritably. "It would be a waste of money, Papa."

"Oh, if you think so, my dear," Louis said, amenable to his eldest daughter's opinion.

Thérèse opened her mouth to protest that she was certain she would make splendid progress under careful instruction, but Papa was asking Marie if she had remembered to order the flour.

"Sacrifice is pleasing to God," Father Domin had said at the Communion class the previous week.

Thérèse closed her mouth firmly. She would offer this as a sacrifice and not betray by look or word that she would have dearly loved to have lessons in drawing and painting too.

"Going out to play, my little queen?" Louis enquired, as she slipped from her chair.

"To feed the linnets," she said and ran upstairs quickly before her tears betrayed her.

Sacrifice, she thought miserably, was a wonderful thing, but it was incredibly painful to endure.

Her tears were forgotten however when she and Céline sneaked a look at the newspaper a few days later.

Pranzini, at the moment of execution, had seized a crucifix and kissed it passionately.

"I said there would be a sign!" Thérèse cried in triumph. "Our prayers were really answered, Céline. He did repent."

"It certainly looks like it," Céline said slowly.

"Oh, I can hardly believe it!" Thérèse's blue eyes were shining. "To save souls from going to hell by prayer and sacrifice—I shall make that my chief concern from now on!"

She would have liked to do something noble and spectacular, but they were all going to Uncle Isidore's for supper and the only sacrifice possible there was to sit quietly and eat whatever was put in front of one. Thérèse hated eating in company. Her throat closed up when she tried to swallow and she became all thumbs when she tried to handle her knife and fork. Her uncle, glancing at her, said in an audible aside to Louis,

"Poor little Thérèse seems to be growing quite clumsy these days. You should encourage her to mix more in society."

"My flower doesn't prosper in alien soil. She is happier at home," Louis made excuse.

"She used to be such a bright little soul," Uncle Isidore said. "Now she seems to me to be far too shy and withdrawn. What games do you play, Thérèse?"

"I like reading," she mumbled, blushing scarlet under his kindly but critical regard.

"You should get out into the air more," Aunt Elisa said. "Louis, tell us how Pauline is. She will be making her final vows soon, won't she?"

"On the day that Thérèse makes her first Holy Communion," Louis said. "I tell you, Elisa, that will be a wonderful day for us all!"

Thérèse, glad that attention had shifted from her, finished her pudding without clattering her spoon against the side of the dish. The rest of the evening would be much more to her liking, with Papa and Uncle Isidore singing duets together and Aunt Elisa and Cousin Jeanne telling riddles. Cousin Marie, who was delicate, sat on the couch near the fire with a rug over her legs. She was a spoilt minx, Louis said privately, forever demanding her own way and threatening to have a headache or a stomach-ache if she didn't get it. After a moment Thérèse stole across to sit with her, shaking her head when Jeanne asked her if she wanted to join in the big family jigsaw they were all working on. She loved jigsaws but they gave poor Cousin Marie a headache.

Sacrifice, Thérèse thought wistfully, got more difficult the more that one practised it. She smiled at her cousin who said pettishly,

"Do move to one side. You're blocking all the light off me."

"I'm sorry," Thérèse said meekly. She was tempted to give her cousin a sly pinch, but reminded herself sternly that such behaviour was not the way to win jewels for a heavenly crown.

Those making their first Communion spent the three days before in retreat at the school. Louis had been reluctant to allow Thérèse to go, for she had never slept away from the family in her life, but Marie said firmly,

"You must allow her to do as the other girls do, Papa. They will regard her as a baby if you don't."

"We will come and see you every evening," he whispered to Thérèse. "You won't cry too hard, will you?"

Thérèse had no intention of crying at all. She was more excited than she had ever been in her life before.

Only a few days of instruction and meditation and then she would be walking up the aisle in the lovely dress of white silk and the short lace veil that Marie had sewed so patiently. Papa had made her a little gold watch that pinned to the yoke of her dress; Sister Agnes had sent her an hourglass and Céline had painted a picture for her of a little white flower growing at the door of a golden tabernacle, and Léonie had made a bright blue sash to tie over her shoulder as a sign that she had now joined the Association of Angels to which all the new communicants were privileged to belong.

As Marie packed her case, she found it impossible to keep

still, but hopped from one leg to the other.

"We will go and see Sister Agnes after the ceremony, won't we?"

"Yes, of course."

"Will she wear the roses we sent? I put a little note in to say that they must be sprinkled with water and kept in a cool place. Marie, what am I going to say in Confession on the eve? I have so many faults I shall never get through them!"

"Faults are not important," Marie said. "Just tell the priest that you wish to learn how to love God more and more deeply. That will be better than making long lists of all the bad things that you think you've done. Now go and kiss Léonie and remember to thank her again for the sash."

Thérèse did as she was bade, hugging Léonie until the older girl almost overbalanced. Léonie was to be her god-mother when she was confirmed the next month. That had been a sacrifice too, because secretly she would have preferred Marie, but Papa had reminded her that Léonie would come of age in June and it would please her immensely to be Thérèse's sponsor.

"The bishop will slap your cheek as a symbol of what you must be prepared to suffer for the Faith," Marie had told her, "and then he will trace a cross upon your forehead, and you will be a full member of Christ's Church."

Confirmation was certainly something to look forward to eagerly, but Holy Communion had about it the essence of something personal. It would be like falling in love, Thérèse thought, and the Lover would never die, or grow old, or desert her. She would be safe in an undying, unvarying affection, caught like a little fish in the gleaming net of the Fisherman.

At the Abbey the long dormitory with its rows of white curtained beds enchanted her. The older boarders had been

72

moved out to make room for the Communion retreat. There would be talks and tests and meditations. Thérèse hadn't the faintest notion how to meditate. Left to herself she liked to drift into a half dream where birds sang under the wide blue arch of heaven and there was no more death or separation.

"Surely a great girl of eleven can do her own hair!" the nun in charge exclaimed when, on the first morning, Thérèse presented herself, comb in one hand and hair-ribbons in the other.

"My big sister always does it," Thérèse said shyly. "Come along then." The nun held out her hand for the comb and began to pull the knots out of the child's tangled curls with such impatience that Thérèse felt that her hair was being tugged out by the roots.

There was a parcel waiting for her when they trooped down to the refectory for breakfast.

"Your sister, Léonie, brought it. She said it was a little extra gift from her," the nun said.

Thérèse unwrapped it eagerly and exclaimed with joy. "Léonie has given me her own crucifix," she said. "It's the big one that always hangs over her bed! Oh, what a lovely thing to do!"

It was a very large crucifix but she couldn't bear to be parted from it for an instant, so she tucked it firmly into her sash.

"Just like your sister at Carmel," Father Domin said solemnly when she trotted into the first class in the morning. "I hope your answers to my catechism test justify the ornament you're wearing."

Thérèse would have liked to explain that she was not wearing it as an ornament but as a symbol of all the martyrdoms she was willing to endure, but the priest was already rapping for silence and the chance was lost. She took her seat and fixed her eyes solemnly on Father Domin.

The three days of the retreat passed more quickly than she had expected. Papa came every evening with her sisters and she was permitted to take them round the grounds for a walk. She showed them the bird cemetery that she had made, and Papa was very complimentary, declaring it was the prettiest graveyard he had ever seen in his life.

The morning dawned cloudless and warm, with a faint breeze scenting the air. Thérèse sprang out of bed more quickly than she had ever moved before, and stood like a small white-gowned sprite, curling up her toes against the rough matting that covered the floor.

Her new white dress, her veil, and the blue sash were laid over the chair at the bottom of the bed. Some of the bigger girls had come to help them into their dresses and to comb hair into braids and curls and fringes. Thérèse was shivering a little for excitement had wrought her to the highest pitch.

The church was crowded with relatives. She supposed that Papa was there, with Marie, Léonie and Céline in their Sunday dresses and spring hats, but she kept her eyes lowered and her hands clasped like the other girls as they walked in pairs down the aisle. The singing of the choir soared up into the vault of the roof and the altar was a blaze of gold and crimson.

Every second of the ceremony was impressed upon her mind, but it was impossible to explain afterwards how she felt.

Marie had told her a story once about a white stone on which a person could read their true name, the name known only to Heaven and bestowed upon them at the moment of creation. Now she read her name on the white stone and the knowledge of it shivered to her soul.

"The poor little thing is crying," Jeanne whispered to Aunt Elisa. "Do you think she is missing Pauline?"

"She is smiling," Aunt Elisa murmured back. "She is happy. Our Thérèse weeps on every occasion."

Thérèse heard no whispering. She was aware only of the singing in her heart and the whiteness of the lilies with their golden stamens and cool green leaves.

"Now we go to Carmel to see Pauline become the bride of Christ," said Papa, bending to wipe her face with his big pocket handkerchief. "Her Clothing was her betrothal in a manner of speaking and now comes her wedding day. She will be happy to see you in your lovely dress, and hear how you felt as soon as you had received the Blessed Bread."

"You wore my crucifix," Léonie whispered, hugging her. "I was so pleased to see it."

"And Victoire has baked a splendid iced cake especially in your honour," Céline announced. "There is to be a party tonight with jelly shapes and coloured lanterns. Oh, you did look lovely in your dress, Thérèse, I heard one of the ladies behind us ask who the angel was, and I am certain that she meant you for you had only just passed by. Don't you feel happy today?"

"Too happy to speak of it," Thérèse said.

As they walked along her feet scarcely seemed to touch the ground and the air itself seemed to rain gold down on her beribboned head.

SIX

"I tell you frankly, Louis, that child will be ill again unless she has a complete change of scene," Isidore said bluntly.

"Thérèse seems very quiet and contented," Louis said. "She never gives us a moment's trouble, you know, and her marks at school are always remarkably high."

"She is too quiet," Isidore said. "When I talk to her these days she shrinks away and blushes crimson as if I were going to eat her."

"She's at a difficult age," Louis said vaguely.

"If you had more worldly experience you would know that all females are always at a difficult age," Isidore said wryly. "Now, to return to Thérèse, why don't you let her and Céline come to Trouville with us next month? You are going away yourself, aren't you?"

"To Constantinople," Louis looked unhappy at the prospect. "I wish it were not necessary, but there is nobody else I can trust to value stones properly and offer a fair price for them. When this transaction is concluded I intend to realize my assets and retire."

"Meanwhile a trip will benefit you as greatly as it will benefit Thérèse. Marie and Léonie are capable of managing everything at home for a week or two. It would make their task even easier if they didn't have to worry about the young ones."

"It's very good of you, Isidore," Louis said gratefully. "We owe you a great deal, the girls and I. I will tell Thérèse this evening and give her a little time to prepare herself."

76

To his surprise, Thérèse, instead of weeping at the prospect of going away from home, greeted his news with pleasure.

"Les Buissonets is not the same when you're absent from it, Papa," she said. "It will be good to go to Trouville."

"Your uncle thought you looked in need of a change. There is nothing worrying you, sweetheart?"

"The fear of sunburn," she said merrily.

"Vain puss!" He hugged her, deciding that his brother-in-law had been mistaken. Nothing ailed Thérèse at all.

I lied by omission, Thérèse thought, going to her garden plot and beginning to water it with every sign of energetic enjoyment. I ought to have told him that for weeks now I've been so troubled and uneasy that I don't know which way to turn. But if I had told him then I would have been guilty of piling my own troubles onto him and that would have made him more anxious about going away and leaving me than he is already.

She glanced up at the sky, noticing with dismay that heavy rain clouds had begun to form. That meant she had already wasted a whole can of water on blossoms that would soon be thoroughly wetted all over again. It was impossible to live for more than a few minutes without committing a sin.

There were mornings when she woke and the sadness of the day ahead rushed in and swamped her. There was the misery of school to be endured where her classmates either ignored or teased her. She wished passionately that she could make friends as Céline did. It was a sin to strive for the love of one's fellow creatures. They were all fickle, blowing now hot now cold. She preferred the company of her linnets and canaries because they were always glad to see her and never called her Cry Baby or tried to trip her up with their skipping ropes.

"The big girls haven't been bullying you, have they?" Céline asked one day, coming upon her wiping away tears in the playground. "If they have, you just tell me and I'll settle them."

Céline had looked so resolute that Thérèse had been tempted, but it was wicked to tell tales and get others into trouble, so she had assured her that nothing was wrong. That had been a lie too, and she had agonized over it for the rest of the day.

It was such a relief to come home at the end of the afternoon, to be greeted with hugs and kisses from the rest of the family, but it was terrible to think how they would shrink away from her if they knew how black with sin her soul was. She had tried to explain how she felt to Marie, but the latter, brushing her hair briskly, said,

"There's nothing wrong with your soul, except a bad case of scruples. You should accept the fact that we all have faults and it does no good at all to dwell on them."

But it was impossible not to dwell on them. Thérèse found she was watching her own actions with such intensity that she was afraid to open her mouth lest she say something wrong, nervous of performing the smallest act lest it be an occasion for sin.

"Go and enjoy your holiday," Marie said, kissing her as they left for the station. "I want to see you come back with a happy smile on your lips and all your silly fears quietened."

She had not expected to enjoy herself at all, but the journey was full of interest with travellers getting on and off at the various stops and her aunt producing a packed lunch out of a wicker basket.

The Guérins had taken a house near the quieter end of the bustling little seaside town. From the window of her bedroom Thérèse could look out over a sandy beach with the sea rippling beyond it. The water was blue from a distance, green and grey when one stood at the edge and looked down into it. There were deep rock pools, long trails of shiny brown seaweed sparkling with salt, and little scuttling red crabs.

She was enchanted with everything. Aunt Elsa had bought them all shrimping nets and big straw hats to keep the sun off, and with her shoes and stockings off, Thérèse skipped in and out of the white laced waves that frilled the edge of the sea and scrunched the damp sand between her bare toes.

There were picnics on the cliffs above the town when they sat about on the grass and made wreaths out of the young daisies and donkey rides up and down the beach with Uncle Isidore cheering them on and Aunt Elisa sitting under a big, striped umbrella with her knitting fallen unheeded to her lap while she watched the fun.

Poor Cousin Marie was too delicate to join in everything but sat in the shade, a handkerchief over her head and another in her hand, for she was prone to burst into tears at the slightest excuse for all that she was a big girl of fifteen. Thérèse looked on in astonishment when her cousin sobbed bitterly and the entire family rushed about, offering various remedies and trying to cheer her up.

At Les Buissonets such behaviour was tactfully ignored and Thérèse's own fits of crying were saved for her private moments. It would be rather pleasant, she thought wistfully, to lie on a couch and have a great fuss made of her.

Her opportunity came at the end of a long day spent exploring the local countryside. Her legs ached with tiredness and she had a splitting headache. Dropping into an armchair, Thérèse drew a quivering breath and burst into noisy tears.

"For heaven's sake, what ails the child?" Aunt Elisa

demanded, dropping her bonnet as she hurried to investigate. "Have you got a stomach ache, pet?"

Thérèse shook her head and cried harder.

"Have you quarrelled with Céline?" Cousin Jeanne asked.

"No." Thérèse spluttered the word through her sobs.

"Then what is it? Are you missing your Papa?" Aunt Elisa enquired.

"I have a headache," Thérèse wailed truthfully. "My head is hurting so hard that it feels as if it's going to drop off!"

"She is saying that because Marie had a migraine attack yesterday," Jeanne said impatiently. "It's very wrong to cry 'wolf', because nobody will believe you when you're really ill."

"I am ill," Thérèse sobbed indignantly. "I have headaches nearly all the time, but I don't say anything about them. This one is awful."

"Crying won't make it any better," Aunt Elisa scolded. "I think you're being rather a silly little girl. Dry your eyes now and come to supper."

"And don't be so ungrateful," Jeanne put in. "Mamma has gone to a lot of trouble to make your holiday a pleasant one and it's very wrong of you to make such a nuisance of yourself!"

So her attempt to obtain a little fussing had met with failure. It was both puzzling and shaming to find out that when she really had a headache nobody took it seriously. Thérèse blew her nose and choked back her sobs, feeling the tight band of pain round her skull grow even tighter and little towers of coloured light zigzag before her eyes.

But apart from that incident the holiday was a delight. Uncle Isidore gave them some money so that they could buy gifts for Papa, Marie and Léonie, and the Guérin maidservant, Marcelline, took her and Céline into the town to choose their presents.

Thérèse liked Marcelline. She was a big clumsy girl of nineteen, who had been in service with Uncle Isidore and Aunt Elisa since she was thirteen. She had no family of her own and Thérèse tried to be particularly nice to her on that account. It must be a dreadful thing, the child thought, to have no relatives of any kind and to live in someone else's house all the time.

There were some coins left in her purse at the end of the shopping expedition and she bought some chocolates for Marcelline.

"And my favourite flavour!" cried Marcelline. "You're a kind little soul, Miss Thérèse."

"No, I'm not. I'm full of wickedness," Thérèse said sadly. "Aunt Elisa gave me some lovely blue ribbons this morning and I rushed off to find a mirror so that I could see how pretty I looked in them."

"That's not sin," Marcelline said, chuckling. "That's natural in a female. You're going to be a beautiful young lady one day, Miss Thérèse, and some young man might very well come along and think so too."

"Oh, I don't like young men," Thérèse said solemnly.

"You don't know any," Marcelline said. "Have a chocolate."

"No, thank you. I'm not supposed to eat in the street," Thérèse said primly.

"You always do everything you're told, don't you?" Marcelline commented. "I suppose it comes easily to you."

"No, it comes very hard," Thérèse said. "I generally want to do what I ought not to do, but as I love God then I make up my mind to do what He wants."

"I don't love God very much then," Marcelline said. "I must be honest, Miss Thérèse, but I don't feel much for Him at all."

81

"It isn't a question of feeling," Thérèse said slowly. "Loving doesn't mean feeling love, else we'd never be able to love our enemies, would we? I think it means wanting the very best for somebody, and trying to give it to them. That's loving, as I see it."

"It's too deep for me," Marcelline said, shaking her head and helping herself to another chocolate. "I tell you, Miss Thérèse, I sometimes think that you won't last long on this earth. The things you say!"

"Oh, it would be nice to go up to Heaven very quickly," Thérèse agreed. "When I was little I used to hope that we would all die very soon and fly up together. Of course I was very young then."

She was a little hurt when Marcelline laughed harder than ever, but consoled herself with the thought that not everybody understood her as did Marie or Sister Agnes.

The holiday over they returned to Les Buissonets where Marie and Léonie were waiting to exclaim with pleasure over their gifts. Papa was expected back in a few days and there was a flurry of sweeping and polishing in readiness for his return.

"And before we know it you will be back at school," Marie said. "Victoire will have to walk to school with you now that Céline is leaving."

"Leaving!" Thérèse's blue eyes were round with horror. "But Céline cannot possibly leave school!"

"My love, Céline is sixteen now," Marie said. "She cannot stay on at the Abbey for ever."

School without Céline would be an unendurable purgatory. Though they were not in the same class it had been a comfort to know that Céline was in the same building and could occasionally be glimpsed at playtime. Now she would be entirely alone, with nobody to care when she was teased by the others or left to wander about the grounds without any invitation to join in the games.

"If you make me go back to school without Céline I shall die!" she cried dramatically.

"No you won't. You'll settle in very nicely and get high marks just as you always do," Marie said briskly, "and in January, when you are thirteen, you will be eligible to join the Children of Mary Association. Now you know how you've been looking forward to that."

It was true, but it didn't make the prospect of returning to school any easier. Left to himself Papa would have allowed her to do her lessons at home, she was certain, but just as he had never countermanded any of Pauline's decisions, so he never went against Marie.

"My princess must be a brave girl and go back to school," he said firmly. "You like the lessons, don't you?"

She liked most of the lessons, especially history and science. There were all kinds of new inventions that she wanted to learn about, and more books than she could count that she longed to read. The trouble was that she was sure she ought to spend less time reading and more time praying. She tried to discipline herself to break off in the middle of a sentence and say the rosary instead. Every good Catholic venerated the rosary devotion, but Thérèse found it terribly dull to go on and on repeating the Hail Mary while her small fingers kept tally on the beads. Her mind wandered off in all directions and sometimes she even fell asleep in the middle and lost count altogether. It was becoming harder and harder to cope with the guilt that weighed down her mind and heart. Life had become a quagmire of temptations into which she blundered at every turn, and when she made her Confession she came away uncomforted.

"If you tell the priest every little thing you imagine you've done wrong he'll never get the opportunity to hear

83

anybody else," Marie said. "You are to think of three faults and confine yourself to those, and I'll take the rest on my own shoulders."

Dear, kind, sensible Marie, with her lively ways. It was impossible to imagine life without her. But Marie was often busy with the household duties and had less time to spare for her youngest sister than Thérèse needed. Even Papa was often too busy for more than a quick hug and a few kind words. He was winding up his jewellery and watch-making business and that meant frequent trips into town and whole days poring over account books up in the belvedere.

Thérèse didn't like to disturb him too often, and frequently hung about on the stairs waiting for him to emerge, only to be told crossly by Léonie that she was wasting time.

Léonie was frequently out of temper, Thérèse thought sadly. The tantrums of her girlhood had settled into sullenness, and she seemed restless and dissatisfied, forever rushing off to see Uncle Isidore and Aunt Elisa.

Even Céline was changing. Everybody said what a pretty young woman she was becoming, with her long pale hair swept up into an elaborate roll and her skirts lengthened to the ground. She went about a lot with Cousin Jeanne to parties and socials and when Thérèse tried earnestly to warn her against earthly vanities she laughed and told her not to be a prig.

"We are all growing up, Thérèse. It's time that you did the same."

But Thérèse didn't want to grow up if growing up meant change. And she herself was becoming different. There were changes in her body that she couldn't help noticing and her fits of crying were becoming more prolonged and more difficult to conceal.

"The child needs dancing lessons," Aunt Elisa said. "My

84

own Marie is so much better in health and spirits since she went to dancing classes."

Dancing lessons were worse than anything yet devised. They were held twice a week in an upstairs room at the Abbey, with Miss Delarue thumping away at the piano in one corner, and two lines of girls solemnly curtseying to one another and beginning the Step-One-Two-Three, Step-One-Two-Three, that must have been the most fiendish torture ever devised, Thérèse thought.

"Mademoiselle Martin, do not look at your feet! Smile at your partner. Dip and glide dip and glide. Remember that you are dancing with a handsome young man."

Thérèse looked gloomily at her partner, a big girl who dragged her around the floor as if she were a dead weight. It was impossible to imagine her as a handsome young man, and anyway she didn't like boys. Apart from Papa and Uncle Isidore she didn't know any young men at all, and she felt no desire to remedy the omission. Boys were even rougher than girls and did dreadful things like pulling wings off flies. Thérèse had been on her way home from school one afternoon and some boys had whistled after her and called, "Hello, darling!"

Thérèse had frozen with terror, even the tiny hairs at the back of her neck prickling, and walked past them without turning her head or altering her pace, though her heart was beating so rapidly, that she could scarcely breathe.

It was safer to stay at home where she was left in peace to feed her birds and tend her flowers. Les Buissonets was the loveliest place in the world and she loved every inch of it.

"My dear child, cannot you explain to me what troubles you," Father Domin asked in kindly concern, looking down at her as she sat hunched over her desk.

"I don't feel very well," she mumbled.

"But you never feel very well," the priest said. "Sister tells me that you spend most of your time being treated in the infirmary for headaches and stomach aches. Is something troubling you?"

"Only myself," said Thérèse and burst into a storm of weeping.

Father Domin must have spoken to Papa because, a few days later, he took her aside and said,

"Princess, are you really miserable at school?"

"More than I can begin to tell you," she cried. "I hate it there, Papa! It's like being locked up in prison all day."

"Your teachers will be sorry to lose you because your marks are so high and your conduct exemplary."

"But I could do lessons at home," she begged.

"What about the Children of Mary? You won't be allowed to join unless you spend a certain amount of time at school."

"I could go in for the sewing class on two afternoons a week," Thérèse said eagerly. "I wouldn't mind doing that."

"Your uncle tells me there is a widowed lady in town, a Madame Papinau, who would be willing to tutor you."

"Cannot Marie teach me?"

"Madame Papinau lives with her mother in somewhat reduced circumstances," he explained, "and the money for your tuition would benefit her greatly. She could instruct you every morning, and then twice a week you have your sewing lesson and the dancing class—oh, there will be no lack of occupation for you. No time for these silly bouts of crying and nervous headaches."

Even dear Papa didn't fully understand, Thérèse thought sadly, but then Papa himself was not always very well these days. He had recently been stung by a horse fly and his neck was so inflamed that the doctor had recommended leeches to draw out the infected blood. They had all had a bad fright when he had had a kind of fainting fit just after a meal, and had come out of it mumbling in a confused manner. Since then she had noticed that he was apt to drag his leg a little after he had been walking any distance.

She would have to make do with Madame Papinau's instruction and not worry him unduly. He was after all sixty-three years old, an advanced age for her thirteen year old eyes.

Madame Papinau, however, proved to be gentle and charming, with a large, amiable cat that sat on Thérèse's knee and shared her lessons. She was enchanted with her pupil and often interrupted the lessons to bring in visitors who would lavish praise on the dainty child with her long ringlets and vivid blue eyes. It was delightful not to be turned out to play with a crowd of shouting girls. Now, at midmorning break, she sipped hot chocolate and listened to old Madame Cochain ramble on about her girlhood.

Twice a week she went back to the Abbey, slipping into the back row of the sewing class and working away quietly until the bell rang. The other Children of Mary had brought games and sweets to share, but nobody took any notice of Thérèse so she crept into the chapel, ate the jam sandwiches that Victoire had made, and then had a little nap in front of the tabernacle. She always went in with the intention of confessing the black state of her soul, but after a few minutes her eyelids would droop and she would wake without having dreamed but feeling more at peace with herself and the rest of the world.

SEVEN

They were packing in readiness for their annual fortnight in Alençon. Marie was giving final instructions to Victoire who would remain behind to look after the house while the family was away, and Léonie was helping Louis to put his books in order, a task which she enjoyed more than reading their contents. Céline had gone round to Uncle Isidore's and had offered to take Thérèse with her, but the youngest girl preferred to tidy up her own study. It was Pauline's old attic room and, strictly speaking, belonged to all the girls but by degrees Thérèse had made it her own.

She had furnished it to her taste with a large black cross on one wall, a basket of dyed grasses on another, a portrait of Pauline on the third, with the birdcage below it. A table of white marble held a statue of Our Lady with Thérèse's lesson books piled about it, a table covered with a green cloth and holding a statue of St Joseph, a watchcase, an hour glass, and several vases of flowers, a couple of chairs and a doll's cot comprised its contents. Thérèse's ideal was a perfectly tidy and fragrant room but it was an ideal seldom realized, for she was apt to begin clearing up her papers and leave the task half way through because something more interesting had occurred to her to do. In consequence the attic often resembled a jumble sale, with a clutter of work boxes, shell and raffia baskets, half-finished drawings, and tangled skeins of embroidery silk.

She was halfway through clearing and had come across a set of picture cards with the alphabet on them, too young for a big girl of thirteen but suitable for younger children, when Marie's firm step was heard on the stair and there was a tap on the door.

"I've nearly finished," Thérèse scrambled up from her knees. "I think that I'll get all my old toys together before Christmas and give them to the poor children at the Orphanage. Do you think that's a good idea?"

"Very commendable," Marie said, but her tone was somewhat abstracted and she bit her lip uncertainly as she glanced at her sister.

"Is something wrong?" Thérèse, sensitive to the other's mood, looked enquiring.

"Sweetheart, I've something to tell you," Marie sat down and drew the child nearer.

"Is something wrong? Is Papa too unwell to go on holiday?"

"Nothing is wrong," Marie assured her. "It is merely that I have something to tell you that may upset you."

"I'm not going back to school," Thérèse said, setting her lips in a tight line.

"No, no. You must continue your studies with Madame Papinau," Marie said. "She's very pleased with the application to your lessons that you display. No, it is not bad news, not if you consider it calmly."

"Then what?" Thérèse raised worried blue eyes, her fingers gripping one another in expectation of a blow.

"I have decided to enter Carmel," Marie said.

The blow was so much greater than she had feared that Thérèse stared dumbly, all the colour leaving her cheeks.

"It's not a sudden decision," Marie said, speaking rapidly now that the first hurdle was passed. "I have been turning the matter over in my mind for months."

"But you don't want to become a nun," Thérèse managed to stammer. "You've never even mentioned the possibility——"

"Every vocation is slightly different, I suppose," Marie said. "Pauline made up her mind when she was still a girl and never wavered from it, but in me the ambition has worked secretly like yeast. I couldn't believe that it was happening. I told myself that it was foolish, that I didn't really want to leave the world at all, but that was even more foolish, to try and ignore what was happening inside me."

"But how will we manage?" Thérèse asked in a small voice. "You're our mother now that Pauline has become Sister Agnes."

"There is Léonie. She is quite capable of running a house."

"But Léonie isn't you," Thérèse said unhappily. "I am very fond of her but it won't be the same. You know it won't be the same!"

"Nothing ever stays the same," Marie said. "You have to learn that. I might have met a young man and left you to get married and start a family of my own, you know, but I never felt the slightest desire to be married. I suppose I've had a vocation for a long time and not realized it. Papa and the others were not as surprised as I imagined they would be."

"You've told them already?" Thérèse looked at her in hurt astonishment.

"Only because I wanted to tell you quietly when we were by ourselves."

"When will you go?" Thérèse asked shakily.

"After we return from Alençon I will enter as a postulant. Mother Prioress has already accepted me and says I am to be known as Sister Marie of the Sacred Heart, so I won't be changing my name as Pauline did."

"But I will be going into Carmel myself in a year or two. Couldn't we wait and go together?" Thérèse begged.

"Oh, not that silliness again!" Marie made a little impatient gesture and stood up. "Why, even if you were not far too young to decide on such an important matter, it would break Papa's heart to lose you. You know you've always been his favourite!"

"I won't be able to bear it," Thérèse said, abandoning any pretence of dignity and beginning to cry helplessly. "It will be like losing Pauline all over again. Please don't go, Marie. Please think about it! I shall be ill. I know I shall be ill."

"I will be very sorry and anxious if you are," Marie said, "but it won't alter my mind. Now finish tidying up your things and come downstairs, and try not to cry too much. You will feel quite different about it in time."

But Thérèse was certain she wouldn't. Nothing would ever be the same again when Marie had gone. Léonie was very helpful these days and eager to please but she didn't have the strength or wisdom of either Sister Agnes or Marie.

The attic room with its cheerful clutter had always been Thérèse's refuge. She loved to spend hours here with her books and birds and her own thoughts for company, but it was all spoiled now. Nothing could ever be the same. Thérèse began to cry more noisily, but the door had closed and Marie's step dwindled away on the stair.

That was the most dismal holiday they had ever spent. She could never look back on it afterwards without a shudder.

To begin with she had to endure constant references to Marie's vocation for Louis insisted on taking them round to see all their old friends so that his daughter could make her farewells and Thérèse had to hold back shaming public tears as Marie was congratulated and Louis told how blessed he was in the giving of two daughters to Carmel.

'Three', Thérèse wanted to cry. 'I am going into Carmel too. I was the first one who wanted to go, for I've always known that one day I would be a nun'.

Nobody would have listened, so she sat, head lowered to conceal her brimming eyes, and wished the visit was at an end.

There was not even any consolation when they went to Zélie's grave. Thérèse had picked a big bunch of cornflowers to put on it, but at the last moment she left them behind in the boarding house, and Papa refused to turn back for them because it was already spotting with rain. By the time they reached the graveyard it had become a downpour and they huddled miserably under their umbrellas while Louis said the rosary. Thérèse's beads were cold and wet between her chilled fingers and when she glanced at Marie, her sister looked already remote and indifferent to her small concerns.

But the worst didn't happen until the very last day of the holiday. Thérèse and Céline came down to breakfast to find Papa seated at the table with his head in his hands while Marie paced up and down with her skirt swishing and her eyes furious.

"Shall I tell them, Papa, or will you?" she demanded, swinging around as the two girls came in.

"It is Léonie." He raised his head wearily. "She has entered the Poor Clare Convent here."

"Without one word to anybody," Marie said tightly. "She was not in her bed when I woke up, but I assumed she had gone to early Mass and left me to lie in. I found a note, propped up on the dressing table, if you please!"

"She tells us she made up her mind long ago to become a nun, but decided to enter at once," Marie said angrily. "It was deceitful of her. Utterly deceitful!"

"But who will keep house for us if Léonie isn't there?"

Thérèse asked.

The thought that Marie might stay at home flashed into her mind, but it was quenched as Louis said.

"This must make no difference to your own plans, my dear. Céline will manage beautifully I'm sure."

"You're not going to allow her to stay!" Marie exclaimed. "A matter like this needs to be discussed by the elders of the family and your permission gained. We must go round and bring her home at once."

"My love, Léonie is twenty-three years old and doesn't need permission to do what is in her mind," Louis said gently.

"Mind! Léonie never had a mind!" Marie exploded, "No, Papa, I'm very sorry to sound uncharitable, but you know it's true. Why, she still has great difficulty in reading and writing. She's always been queer tempered and difficult, full of fads and fancies. This is simply another example of it."

"In which case she will come home of her own accord, and our scolding will only confirm her more obstinately in her present decision," he said. "We will all go round to see her but not to drag her away against her will. We will make it clear that we love her dearly and want her to be happy."

Louis seldom spoke with such decision but, when he did, his daughters listened. Marie subsided, though her quick breathing and clenched fists betrayed her continuing temper.

Thérèse found it impossible to eat any breakfast. What had happened was so surprising that it seemed unreal. As they walked to the Convent she found herself wondering if they would even recognize Léonie when they saw her, or if some extraordinary change had taken place in her overnight.

"The nuns wouldn't have questioned her arrival," Louis

said, "for they know our family well. When you were very tiny, Thérèse, I used to take you fishing with me and then we'd take our catch to the Poor Clare nuns."

"A pity you bothered," Marie muttered and fell silent, biting her lip, as her father frowned at her.

The Convent was in a narrow, dark street and Thérèse's heart sank as they followed the portress down a long, dark corridor into a whitewashed room, furnished with a bench, with a grille at one end. It was not unlike Carmel but there was no feeling of warmth or welcome there, and the nun who admitted them jangled her keys impatiently as if she considered their arrival to be an intrusion. Louis went into an inner room to talk with the Prioress and came back to them, looking sadly resigned.

Léonie will come to the grille for a moment," he said. "We must be very kind to her. You hear me, Marie?"

She nodded, her lips compressed, as the shutters rattled back and Léonie looking very young and touching in her habit, stood behind the grille.

"My dear child!" Louis rose and went up to her. "You have already put on the habit."

"I am sorry if it displeases you, Papa," she said in a high nervous voice. "I did what I believed was best, but it wasn't with the intention of hurting you."

"You must do as your conscience bids," he said gravely. "It has been a surprise to us all—a great surprise and I'll not deny it!"

"It was a shock," Marie said flatly.

"Then I am sorry for it." Léonie flushed, and then said, her voice quivering a little. "Don't be angry, Marie. I never wanted to hurt you either."

"But why a Poor Clare? You could have entered Carmel."

"I wanted to do something different," Léonie said. "I wanted to make an independent decision by myself."

94

"And you truly think it's the right decision?" Marie asked sharply.

"Time alone can tell us that," Louis interposed. "We will all pray for you, sweetheart, and if you find out that this is not the path for you I can come to fetch you home at a moment's notice."

"You're very good to me, Papa." Her voice broke and tears glittered on her lashes.

"Come now, pet. Don't spoil your pretty eyes with weeping," he said in distress.

"You had better take a good, long look at them then," she answered, half-laughing, "because the Rule forbids us to raise them in public when we have taken our final vows."

"Oh, I wish you had waited to say a proper goodbye to us," Thérèse said wistfully.

"When the Lord calls us we have to accept the call at once," Louis said.

"Then you do understand, Papa? I had to do it this way," Léonie said.

Her eyes pleaded with Marie but the other gazed steadfastly at the floor as if she, not Léonie, had taken vows.

"I have to go now. They are very strict about visitors," Léonie said.

"You go with our love and my blessing," Louis said. "You must do what you believe to be right, but I wish you had mentioned it. We none of us thought for a moment that you were considering such a step."

"None of you ever asked me what I wanted to do," Léonie said, a bitter note in her voice.

The memory of that stayed with Thérèse when they left the gloomy convent. She found herself remembering all the little kindnesses that Léonie had done for her, regretting all the times she had turned aside or run off to find one of the others when Léonie had wanted to talk to her.

"I cannot delay my entering into Carmel," Marie repeated, "whatever Léonie has taken it into her head to do."

"Of course not, my dear Marie." Louis leaned across and patted her hand. "We must prepare for the great day as soon as we reach home."

But it was not a great day at all, Thérèse thought miserably when a month later she embraced Marie at the door of the enclosure. It was an awful, lonely occasion, with Marie's round face pinched with the effort to hold back tears.

"Be a good girl now, and do as Céline and Papa tell you." Her voice was husky and she pushed Thérèse away almost roughly and went through the door without looking back.

"It's no good my trying to be a mother to you," Céline said regretfully. "There isn't nearly enough difference in our ages."

"Oh, I shall be fourteen in January. I'm too old for a mother," Thérèse said bravely.

Her manner evidently convinced Céline who went off happily to experiment with a recipe book in the kitchen.

Thérèse slipped into Marie's bedroom and stood, looking round at the unnaturally tidy room with all Marie's possessions neatly stacked away. In this room she had been so ill that it seemed as if her whole being had splintered into pieces. In this room the Holy Virgin had smiled at her. Or had it been an illusion, the dream of a sick mind? She knelt in front of the statue, gazing up at the calm, carved features. The eyes stared ahead sightlessly and indifferently. Thérèse's own eyes filled with fresh tears and she began to sob bitterly. Pauline and Marie were both gone now, and Léonie was in Alençon at a gloomy convent where the nuns didn't seem to be in the least pleased to see one. She had promised to be a good, brave girl and not cry, but it was impossible to help it when all the people in her small world were leaving her.

Nothing was as it had been before. When they went to the parlour of Carmel on Wednesdays, Sister Agnes and Sister Marie greeted them behind the grille, their voices decorous and subdued, and there were few traces of Pauline or Marie in the quiet faces. They were in their right place, Thérèse thought, but when, in the few minutes alone with them that she was permitted, she tried to raise the subject of her own vocation, she received scant encouragement.

"You're too young to even think about it," Sister Marie said. "That's always been my opinion and I've found no reason to alter it since I came in here. This is a life of mature reflection, not for a child."

"It might be more sensible if you waited for a few years," Sister Agnes said. "There is no guarantee that you would be allowed to remain in this particular Carmel anyway. You would probably be sent to another convent."

Thérèse wanted desperately to explain that it didn't matter. She wasn't entering in order to be near her sisters, but because she had been drawn to the contemplative life for years, but tears prevented her from speaking and the sand in the hour glass had run out, marking the end of the visit.

"We must make this a happy Christmas for Papa," Céline said, as the winter closed in, wet and windy.

"It won't be the same without the others," Thérèse said. "I wish I'd been nicer to Léonie when she was here. We always did leave her out of things, you know."

As it happened her regrets were untimely. A few days before the festival, Leonie came home, thin and pale and weeping bitterly.

"It was too hard," was all she could say, shaking her curly head over and over again. "It was so cold and lonely.

So lonely that it bites through to the bone!"

"A breakdown," Uncle Isidore said. "You must let Léonie spend Christmas with us. She will have peace and quiet and fewer things about to remind her of Pauline and her own failure."

"It showed courage to admit that she made a mistake," Louis said.

"Indeed it did," Isidore agreed, "but it is a little fun the girl needs now, not forgiveness."

So Léonie went to stay with Uncle Isidore and Aunt Elisa, and Céline and Thérèse tried valiantly to brighten up the house with silver tinsel and holly sprayed with gold. Louis had been deeply disappointed at Léonie's failure to persevere, and though he was very gentle about it, uttering no word of blame, the younger girl sensed his mood.

"I'll leave your shoe by the fireplace as we always do," Céline promised Thérèse as they put on their cloaks for Midnight Mass. "It always cheers Papa up to watch you open your gifts."

Thérèse brightened, resisting the temptation to peep as they went through the hall.

The Mass was, if possible, even more beautiful this year. Staring at the Crib with its carefully arranged figures Thérèse thought that when she became a nun she would like to be known as Thérèse of the Child Jesus. It was a pity that one was not allowed even to hint at a personal preference.

Listening to the high, sweet carolling behind the closed grille, she tried to identify the voices of her sisters, but they were indistinguishable from the rest. Guiltily, she forced her attention back to the service, suppressing a yawn for it was seldom she was permitted to stay up so late.

"No snow this year," Thérèse regretted as they hurried home through the dark streets. "I do love snow."

"It turns to slush too soon," Louis said hunching his shoulders against the cold.

Victoire was waiting for them with bowls of hot soup already steaming on the table and a fire leaping up the chimney.

Céline and Thérèse started up the stairs together to remove their cloaks while Louis, unwinding his scarf, went into the parlour and glanced down at the decorated and laden shoe. His voice, weary and irritable, reached the two on the landing.

"Thérèse is too big for this childish nonsense. I shall be glad when it's over."

The words were crueller than he had meant them to be, but Céline, tugging at her sleeve, whispered anxiously, "He didn't mean them to be heard. Wait a while before you go down. He'll be so upset if he finds out that he hurt your feelings."

'Hurt' was an understatement. She was wounded to the heart by the sudden, searing thought that she might never have been his favourite child at all, but a little nuisance to be placated with soft words and affectionate lies. Tears closed up her throat and rushed into her eyes.

"Oh, Thérèse." Céline's own eyes were moist with sympathy.

"I'm all right," Thérèse heard herself say, and to her astonishment her voice was bright and gay. "Truly I am. Come! Let's go down and make this a happy Christmas for Papa."

Humming, she ran downstairs and a moment later Louis, his good humour restored, was laughing at her childish prattle as she exclaimed over her gifts. Only Céline, walking more slowly to the parlour, knew that the child Thérèse would never come again.

EIGHT

Louis was seated on the bench, enjoying the mellow warmth of the early evening sun. It had been a beautiful day with a faint breeze in the air to prevent its becoming uncomfortably hot. His leg ached a little, but it was not an entirely unpleasant sensation. Nearby a plump bee investigated a flower and tumbled drunkenly onto the grass. From the dovecot came the full-throated cooing of the birds, and from the open attic window the shriller calls of Thérèse's linnets and canaries.

Thérèse herself had just emerged into the garden and stood, irresolute as if she were poised for flight. He watched her with a kind of wonder, awed by the realization that this slender, glowing creature was his own child. In her blue dress with its ruched apron front and small bustle, her long curls held back by a blue ribbon under a wide straw hat, she looked enchanting. At fourteen and a half she was still small, but the wild rose shading of her cheeks and the brightness of her eyes betokened health.

"Papa." She crossed the lawn and sat down beside him. Glancing at her he saw there were tears glistening on her lashes and her fingers plucked the ends of her sash.

"What is it, princess? What troubles you?" he enquired.

"I have to talk to you, Papa," she said breathlessly.

"Then we'll walk a little." He put his arm about her and they began to pace the shell-bordered path.

"What is it?" he repeated.

"Papa, for years now I have had such a longing in me,"

she burst out. "Ever since I was little I've craved the religious life. I want to enter Carmel as soon as I possibly can."

Deep down he had known what she would say, but her words brought the reality of it home to him.

"You're very young to make such a serious decision," he began.

"Age has nothing to do with years," she said quickly. "Don't you remember when I was little I saw my initial picked out in the stars? I didn't have the words to explain the meaning, but the meaning was already in me. I had a vocation for the religious life even then but I couldn't explain it properly. Now I have the words too, and I have to speak them!"

"Léonie tells me that she too is going to try her vocation again," Louis said. "With the Visitation nuns this time at Caen."

"For me it has been Carmel ever since I first heard of the Order," she plunged on.

"Because Pauline went there? Are you certain it's not that?"

"I would have wanted Carmel even if Pauline and Marie had never entered," she said fervently. "Oh, Papa, if you could only feel a little of the longing that consumes me! But you must feel it because you wanted to be a monk once, didn't you? You must know what it's like to burn with desire for things that are not of this world!"

"Constantly, but God set my feet on a different road," he said. "Your mother too, God rest her soul. He must have loved us both very much to choose our daughters as His brides one by one. But you're still so very young!"

"Papa, listen to me," she pleaded. "I can say this to you because you are the only one who won't scold me for the sin of pride. As soon as I began to be able to think I made up my mind that one day I was going to be a saint. I was determined to be a very great saint. Oh, I didn't know how to go about it. I'm right at the beginning still, but I shall get there one day. And I must take my first step into the enclosure at Carmel."

Louis paused, looking down into her face. Then he turned to pluck a delicate white flower from the border and gave it to her, earth still clinging to its roots.

"The Lord created it," he said slowly, "and nourished it in the soil of home. Will it flourish when it is transplanted?"

"If it is replanted in the soil of Carmel," she whispered. "Give me leave to enter, Papa. I'll never ask you for anything else in my whole life!"

"If your Uncle Isidore gives his consent then I will agree to let you enter Carmel when you are fifteen," he said.

"I'm very grateful to you, Papa," she said in a low voice. "I wish I had more words to express how I feel."

"You and I never needed words, my queen," he said, putting both arms about her and hugging her tightly, but she drew away first, smoothing down her dress, and he knew without being told that she had already begun the journey away from him.

A few days later she stood, shaking with nervousness, before the big, bearded man who looked down at her from under beetling eyebrows and said,

"Child, you must be clean out of your senses to think of such a thing! And Louis must be out of his senses to encourage you in such folly."

"Uncle Isidore, if you would only give your consent—" she pleaded.

"To enter Carmel at fifteen? My dear niece, they don't take babies in convents."

"I am not a baby," she began.

"Neither are you a mature woman," he interrupted. "I am not saying that you have no vocation, love. Your aunt and I have always felt that it was probable you would enter Carmel one day, perhaps even when you were still very young. But not at fifteen!"

"I have been ready to enter since I was nine years old," she said.

"A ridiculous notion," he said flatly. "Speak to me again when you are seventeen. Even seventeen is very young for a vocation, but you are an exceptional person. At seventeen you will have completed you education and gained a little social polish, but I refuse to consider the matter before then."

"Oh, uncle, what will it take to make you change your mind?" she begged.

"A miracle," he said, not without humour, but Thérèse was choking back tears and failed to respond to his smile.

That Uncle Isidore would set his face against her was more than she could bear. Since Christmas she had waited for the opportunity to speak, and now that she had found the courage her own uncle had failed to understand. A miracle, he had said. Very well then, she would go home and pray for a miracle!

"I'll come again tomorrow," she said, with patience struggling with heartbreak so clearly in her voice that he put his arm round her and said kindly, "It is for your own good, my little niece. I'd not hurt you or thwart you for the world, but I am thinking of you."

"And I am thinking of God," she said forlornly. "He's calling me, uncle, and you are calling me back, holding me. Please, Uncle Isidore?"

Her blue eyes entreated him silently, but Jeanne and Céline were coming in together from the garden and their gay voices broke the spell.

Jeanne, having been wooed by most of the young men in Lisieux, had finally settled on an eligible young doctor and wore a handsome diamond to mark her betrothal. Her parents were delighted with her choice and Céline declared that Jeanne would make a beautiful bride. It was very strange, Thérèse thought wistfully, that nobody raised a single objection to Jeanne's marrying a mere human being, but all kinds of barriers were being thrown up to prevent Thérèse from becoming a bride of Christ.

The next day she presented herself even more shiveringly before her uncle, who glanced up briefly from his newspaper and said,

"Well, what brings you here?"

"Uncle?" Her mouth was dry and she swallowed nervously.

"You're not afraid of me, are you?" he demanded.

"Not as a rule," she whispered, licking her lips, "but you can be very alarming."

"Then why do you keep bothering me?" he asked gruffly.

"Because I have to," she said, her words tumbling over one another. "Don't you see, uncle, that I have to come? I prayed all night for you to change your mind."

"I too have prayed," he said abruptly. "Do you know something, Thérèse? Do you know what I have discovered?"

She shook her head.

"I discovered that God doesn't always require prayers if He desires to alter our opinions," he said.

"Alter——?" She stammered the word.

"Your dear aunt and I discussed the matter," Isidore said. "She believes that you were predestined for the contemplative life and that we would be very wrong to stand in your way. So, if you are still of the same mind on your fifteenth birthday, then I'll put forward no more objections."

"Oh, Uncle Isidore! It's been so dark and now you've made it all light again!" she cried.

"Come and give your uncle a kiss then," he said amiably. "And you must promise not to be afraid of me any longer. I am not such an ogre, am I?"

"Only when you sing 'Bluebeard'," she ventured, and laughed at the delight that filled her heart.

It was an excited Thérèse who almost skipped along to the parlour at Carmel a few days later. She had already written to the Prioress and to her two sisters to inform them that both Papa and Uncle Isidore had given their consent to her entering at fifteen.

The grille, however, was shuttered and Father Delatroette rose from a chair to greet them as they entered.

"Monsieur Martin, I trust I find you well?" He shook hands, his eyes darting to Thérèse.

"Well enough, Father." Louis answered with a gentle deference he always displayed towards priests. "My leg troubles me sometimes and I have some numbness in my fingers, but at my age one must expect these little ailments."

"Peace of mind is conducive to health of body," Father Delatroette said, with another meaning glance. "I can imagine your daughter's latest ambition is causing you great anguish."

"Thérèse has wished to enter Carmel for many years," Louis said mildly.

"Children's fancies are not part of the contemplative life," Father Delatroette said. "It's natural that she should want to join her sisters, but it would cause a public scandal if a fifteen year old were to enter Carmel."

"Mother Prioress has expressed herself as willing to take the responsibility," Louis said.

"Mother Prioress is an admirable woman, but even admirable women are not always noted for sensible judgement," Father Delatroette observed. "Fortunately, she has also made it clear that she won't act against the wishes of her Superior, and as Father Superior of the Lisieux Carmel I have decided that fifteen is far too young for any girl, no matter how strong her vocation, to enter any enclosed Order. That is why I am here today. Mother Prioress is naturally distressed at my decision, and has excused herself from parlour."

"But how long must I wait?" Thérèse broke in. She had been listening to Father Delatroette with growing alarm.

"When you are twenty-one, I shall be very happy to give my consent," he said.

"Twenty-one! Oh, you can't mean that!" she cried.

"I am not in the habit of saying what I don't mean," he said.

"But if you knew how I'd prayed, how eagerly I've longed to be a Carmelite!"

"And how prettily you've pleaded, no doubt," he said coldly. "Well, I am neither an indulgent father nor a sentimental nun. I consider the good of the entire Community, not the whims of a schoolgirl."

"Papa!" She swung round, appealing to Louis. "Please do something. Make him understand that I do have a genuine vocation."

"Which you seek to prove by interrupting your elders?" Father Delatroette said.

"I don't mean to be rude," she said, "but I can't accept what you say. I beg you to think about it."

"I've already wasted far too much time on the subject," he retorted. "I know it's a disappointment, but I've spoken my last word on the matter. Come and ask me again when you've reached the age of maturity."

"But there must be someone else to whom we can apply!" she cried.

"There is only the Bishop of Bayeux," Father Delatroette said reluctantly.

"May we not apply to him?" Louis enquired.

"If you wish to go over my head there is nothing I can do to prevent you," the priest said. "Naturally I would abide by his decision, but I can save you a wasted journey now, for His Lordship is not likely to undermine my own authority."

He was holding open the door for them to leave. Louis bowed silently and ushered his now tearful daughter out.

"We will make an appointment to see the Bishop," he said comfortingly. "Don't cry, pet. Léonie leaves for Caen next month, and as soon as she is settled with the Visitation nuns we will make arrangements to go to Bayeux. A personal appeal to His Lordship might tip the scales on our account, but you must prepare for a possible refusal."

He spoke kindly but warningly, his eyes misted with sympathy for her. Since she had confided her ambition to him, he had made her dream his own. When she entered Carmel the chief delight of his existence would be torn away, but something drove him on to demand the sacrifice.

Léonie went hopefully off to Caen. She was returning to the convent where she and the two eldest girls had been educated before Zélie's death, and her memories of the past were so pleasant that her family prayed the future would be equally hopeful for her.

Thérèse's attention was directed towards the forthcoming interview with the Bishop. She had seen him from afar on several occasions but she had never spoken to such an important churchman in her life before.

"He will think I am just a child," she said mournfully to Céline.

"You must put up your hair," Céline said, putting her own head critically on one side. "You can borrow my new hat if you wish, the flat one with the cherries on it. Cherries are very fashionable this season."

On the appointed day, her hair rolled into puffs and Céline's smart white hat, with its sprigs of black and red cherries, anchored to her head with a dozen pins which felt as if they were sticking straight into her brain, Thérèse arrived at the forbidding entrance to the Palace only to be told by a harassed young priest that His Lordship wouldn't be free for another hour.

"We'll wait in the Cathedral," Louis decided. "Come along, Thérèse."

Hand in hand they followed the priest's directions and entered the great, echoing Cathedral. It was packed, evidently for a service, and Louis, beaming proudly at his pretty daughter in her red and white dress and jacket, began to lead her down the aisle towards the front pews where there were one or two vacant seats.

Several heads turned as they passed and Thérèse distinctly heard whispering. With dawning horror she realized that the congregation was garbed in black, that many ladies were veiled and dabbed at their eyes with black bordered handkerchiefs, and that the first words of a Requiem Mass were being intoned.

Louis, smiling happily at the admiration his gaily dressed princess was creating, slowed his footsteps, nodding amiably to any stranger who chanced to catch his eye.

"Papa! Papa!" A Thérèse whose face was as scarlet as the cherries on her hat was tugging him into a side aisle. "Papa, it's a funeral! They will think we are quite mad!"

It was too late to leave without running the gauntlet of staring eyes again. Shaking with silent, hysterical laughter, Thérèse sank to her knees behind a large votive statue and prayed earnestly that she would never meet any of the good citizens of Bayeux again!

The embarrassing incident had at least served to mitigate her nervousness and Thérèse was feeling quite cheerful when they retraced their steps to the Palace.

This time they were admitted at once and shown into a small ante-chamber where a tall, distinguished cleric advanced to shake hands cordially.

"Monsieur Martin and Mademoiselle Thérèse? I am Monsignor Révérony, Vicar General of Bayeux."

"We hoped to see His Lordship," Louis began.

"And so you shall. Please come this way."

He ushered them through a number of small rooms, opening one out of the other, and hung with framed portraits of popes and bishops who frowned down at Thérèse as if she were no bigger than an ant. By the time they had reached a handsomely appointed study with three enormous armchairs set in front of a blazing fire, she had completely forgotten all her carefully rehearsed speeches and could only sink tremblingly to her knees as a bulky figure loomed over her.

"Do sit down, Monsieur Martin." The Bishop waved Louis to one of the armchairs, sat down opposite and gestured to Thérèse to take the centre chair.

"Oh, no, thank you, Monsignor Révérony?" she stammered.

"I thought Carmelites were always obedient," the Vicar General smiled.

"Yes. Yes, of course." She sat down abruptly and was instantly swamped by billowing velvet cushions.

"How may I help you?" the Bishop was asking.

Thérèse shot an anguished look at her father, but Louis was staring down at the carpet as if he were memorizing the pattern.

"My Lord, I want your leave to enter Carmel when I am fifteen," she said at last. In her own ears her voice sounded shrill and piping, but she forced herself to go on. "I know it's an unusual request, but there are those who have early vocations."

"And how long have you had yours?" the Bishop enquired.

"Ever since I can remember," she said earnestly. "I don't mean from when I was born, but certainly since I was three years old. I used to wish we could all die and all go to Heaven at once, but then I heard of the enclosed Orders and I knew that Carmel would be a foretaste of Heaven for me. Not perfect happiness, because we can't expect that down here, but the suffering that will prepare us for the joys in store."

"You have other daughters at the Carmel in Lisieux already, I understand?" the Bishop said, turning to Louis.

"Sister Agnes of Jesus and Sister Marie of the Sacred Heart," he nodded, "and Léonie recently entered the Order of the Visitation at Caen."

"Are you willing to offer a fourth daughter to God?"

"Because God wills it," Louis said simply. "I am certain my daughter has a very strong and deep vocation, and it would be wrong of me to prevent her."

"But you don't really wish to renounce the world before you've seen anything of it, do you?" he enquired.

"I have decided to take Céline and Thérèse on pilgrimage to Rome," Louis interposed.

"Is that the Parish pilgrimage?" Monsignor Révérony asked. "I am its Spiritual Director."

"Yes, I know. We look forward to it very much," Louis said.

"That will be a nice holiday for you, won't it?" the Bishop said coaxingly to Thérèse.

"It will only confirm me in my vocation," Thérèse said.

"My dear child, you're very young," he said. "Your

father and sister would be left alone if you were to enter Carmel. In three or four years time, when you have grown up."

"I put up my hair so that I would look older," she said.

"Oh, I would have taken you for much older than your age," he said solemnly, smoothing his chin with his beringed hand. "But when you enter Carmel they will cut off your pretty hair and dress you in a habit."

"I don't think that's going to trouble me," she said, "because I would be giving up what I had for something better."

"You could lead a mortified life at home," he said.

"I need the discipline of Carmel. It's in Carmel that I will find the suffering to strengthen my soul," she said, tears springing to her eyes.

"Surely those are not diamonds I see there?" the Bishop teased. "Come, that's not how grown up ladies behave!"

"I wouldn't cry so easily if only I were in Carmel," she gulped.

"I'll discuss the matter with Father Delatroette," he said, rising and extending his hand.

"Then my case is already lost," she said dolefully. "Father Delatroette has set his face against my entering Carmel before I'm at least twenty-one. There is nothing in the Rule about that, but he is adamant. Oh, my lord, won't you please reconsider? I want so desperately——"

"Sometimes it does us good to have to wait for what we want, little lady," the Bishop said. "I will reconsider your case. That much I promise. Meanwhile I order you to go to Rome and have a wonderful time there."

He was smiling down at her as she struggled out of the enormous armchair. The hat was giving her a headache and she was convinced her nose was bright red at its tip, but she achieved a faintly wobbly smile.

NINE

November was not the best season of the year for a long trip, but for once Thérèse was not noticing the weather as they left Lisieux on their first stage of their journey to Rome. Their first stop was at Paris where the rest of the party was to gather, but there was time to cram in as much sightseeing as possible before they boarded the train for Italy.

"Perhaps, when you've seen a little of the world, you'll decide to wait before you enter Carmel," Uncle Isidore said hopefully.

Thérèse smiled without answering. Even her uncle didn't understand that the sacrifice of an enclosed life was worth precisely nothing if one disliked the world to begin with.

Meanwhile she enjoyed herself thoroughly, conscientiously visiting every tourist attraction noted in the Guide book, waking in the luxurious hotel room with the prospect of another packed and interesting day ahead. The city with its tree-lined avenues, pavement cafes and steep, huddled roofs fascinated her, as did the people swarming through the streets and boulevards. Ladies in fashionable dresses with sealskin hats and muffs, elegant dandies in top hats and silk lined capes, the flower sellers with their baskets of late blooms, the men in smocks and high leather boots washing down the pavements, the colourful little markets where plump housewives bargained for fruit and vegetables—at every corner there was something new and interesting to observe.

Her most satisfying visit was to the statue of Our Lady of Victories for the statue in Marie's room was a replica of it. Kneeling before it Thérèse was aware of a deep, inner certainty flooding her. The Virgin had really smiled at her. It had not been the illusion of disordered senses but a true and literal event, and her only mistake had been in talking about it.

The others who were to accompany them were what Thérèse thought of as important people, the ladies stylish and gossiping, the gentlemen dropping aristocratic names like confetti when they smoked their after dinner cigars. Rather to her own surprise she discovered that her usual shyness was in abeyance, and she found herself chattering and laughing with perfect composure as the train rattled through scenery of unimaginable beauty.

The mountains, their lower slopes thick with pine, their peaks tinted pastel by the rays of the sun, excited her. Gazing at them she wished she had the talent to write a sublime poem or paint a magnificent picture that would express something of their glory. She would have liked to have had two heads so that she could look out of both windows at once.

As it was, she left Papa dozing in the corner and Céline chatting to their fellow travellers and went along to the observation platform where she could see as much as possible.

"So you are enjoying yourself, Miss Thérèse?" Monsignor Révérony enquired, stepping out to join her.

"The world looks particularly lovely when one is on the point of leaving it," she answered serenely.

"His Lordship the Bishop is not likely to go against the Father Superior," he warned.

"There are higher authorities than the Bishop," she said.

"Hm!" He pulled at his chin, glancing at her with sudden

suspicion, but she was pointing out a village below them, its roofs glittering in the sunshine, a church tower pointing a finger up into the sky.

"Oh, look at that lake! Like a sheet of blue glass!" she cried.

"You seem remarkably happy, despite your recent disappointment," he remarked.

"My own concerns seem very small when I look at all this," Thérèse said earnestly. "I keep reminding myself that if God can create mountains and lakes, then He'll get me into Carmel when it suits Him."

"So you will wait patiently?"

"No, indeed! I'll redouble my efforts and not be so lazy as to expect God to do everything Himself," she exclaimed, laughing.

"Hm!" Monsignor Révérony darted her another suspicious look.

With the glories of the Alps behind them they alighted at the large, noisy Milan terminus. Thérèse had not expected to enjoy Milan, but she was enchanted by the great marble cathedral, climbing up to the very highest of its towers where she and Céline could look down on people and carriages that seemed no bigger than ants. The enormous cemetery was even more interesting with its huge marble statues. Looking at them with awe she remembered the pretty little graveyard she had made at school and wondered if anyone had bothered to carry on the custom.

Venice pierced her with melancholy. The soft plashing of the water against the yellowing walls of the palaces where doges had once ruled, the Bridge of Sighs across which wretched prisoners had once been led to execution, struck her as sad and gloomy. She couldn't understand how the great beauties of the Renaissance had sipped wine and danced through the gilded halls above rat-infested dungeons where fettered prisoners had moaned.

Bologna lacked even the faint charm of Venice. Thérèse, pausing at the open door of the carriage to gaze in dismay at the jostling throng on the platform, was suddenly seized by a pair of masculine arms and whisked down, while a voice exclaimed,

"What a pretty dove I've caught!"

She had never been embraced in her life by anyone except Papa and Uncle Isidore, and her whole being shrank in terror.

"What's your name, darling?" the young man asked. He wore a University gown and spoke French with an execrable accent, but worse than that was the mingled smell of garlic, wine and tobacco and something more, something male and sweaty and compelling that emanated from him.

She tore herself away with such fury that his mouth dropped open in astonishment.

"What is it, princess? Are you hurt?" Louis, who had not seen the incident, hurried up to her anxiously.

"Someone touched me," was all that she could mumble, but her legs were shaking and her heart beating so violently that she felt as if some part of her had been violated. Not until they had settled in at the hotel and she had soaked and scrubbed herself with soapy hot water did she begin to feel clean again, and when she glanced at her father later that evening she could not avoid shuddering. Poor Mamma, to have wanted to enter a convent and been married instead to a creature of flesh and blood who must himself have been forced to indulge in even more intimate contact with her. Marriage was no doubt a vocation for those who were called to it, but Thérèse was devoutly thankful that she was not.

Rome loomed in her mind like a promise that held terror.

They were to spend a week there, though Monsignor Révérony had said that a month would not be sufficient to see all its wonders. Certainly they tried to see as many as possible, attending Mass at a different church each morning and Benediction at a different church each evening, and visiting every possible place of interest in between.

Louis plodded obediently round with the rest of the party, making careful notes of the things he was looking at in his diary, listening earnestly to the briskly professional patter of the guides. His daughters, he was delighted to see, were enjoying themselves enormously, never tiring as they moved from one place of interest to the next, their young faces flushed with cold and exertion.

To actually visit the place where the early Christian martyrs had suffered for their faith had been one of Thérèse's most eagerly awaited treats. She had always thrilled to the idea of martyrdom, to the thought of the high courage needed to face an agonizing death rather than betray their principles.

"And as they waited they sang," she whispered to Céline. "Can you imagine it? Mothers with babies in their arms and men, ordinary working men, all of them saints!"

"You'd need a better imagination than I've got," Céline said, gazing with disappointment over the wooden barrier into the piled rubble that disfigured the arena below. "It looks more like a rubbish tip."

"Couldn't we borrow a ladder? There are some workmen over there."

"They'd think you were off your head or something," Céline disapproved.

"Then we'll climb down." Thérèse cast a furtive glance about and, seeing the rest of the party moving ahead, picked up her skirts and proceeded to follow words with action, shinning over the barrier and scrambling down the piled rocks and stones.

"Thérèse, wait for me!" Céline was following, bruising her hands on the sharp edges of rocks until they both knelt in the space where those first martyrs had shed their blood.

"Girls! Girls, come back at once!" Louis was beckoning them, his gestures impotently frantic.

They climbed back reluctantly, their progress loosening showers of pebbles as they clawed their way up the fallen masonry to emerge, dust covered and triumphant.

"A fine Carmelite you'll make!" Monsignor Révérony chided. "You could very well be excommunicated for breaking the law in such a fashion. This is Italy where women are expected to be ladies."

"Poor, downtrodden creatures, you mean!" she flashed, her grin undeniably infectious. "There are so many rules and regulations about what women can do and cannot do, as if we were inferior to men. I tell you, some men will be in for a nasty shock when they get to Heaven and find out how matters are managed there!"

"I am duly rebuked," Monsignor Révérony said gravely. "Monsieur Martin, you have two young rebels in your family."

"A pair of spirited fillies," Louis agreed, trying to look severe but laughing despite himself.

They were going on to the Church of St Agnes and Thérèse was making a wish with her fingers crossed and her eyes screwed shut the better to concentrate. They had bought souvenirs for the whole family but she had particularly wanted a relic of St Agnes for Pauline.

Only twelve years old, Thérèse thought, and very lovely with golden hair and a handsome young man to court her, but she had betrothed herself to Christ and held firm against all threats and bribes until the Roman centurions had stabbed her in the throat. One little relic would mean so

117

much to Pauline.

She screwed up her eyes even tighter, trying to picture the gently defiant maiden. There was a sharp tinkle at her feet as a small red stone dislodged itself from the tomb and fell to the shining mosaic. Nobody else had noticed it and in a trice it had been thrust deep into Thérèse's purse.

She felt obliged to confess the matter to Monsignor Révérony, but he assured her gravely that nobody would object to her keeping the stone.

"It does seem that St Agnes meant me to have it for my sister," she agreed cheerfully. "St Agnes has always been a great friend of mine, you know. She and St Cecilia are my favourite martyrs, I think."

"Did you know there is no real evidence that St Cecilia ever played or sang in her life, for all that she is patron of music?" he asked.

"Oh, but you mustn't take it literally, Monsignor," she advised. "The music was in her heart, don't you see? Her whole life was a song and she died singing it."

"And how would you choose to die?" he asked lightly.

"Of love," she answered simply. "I want to die of loving, Monsignor. Does that sound foolish?"

"As foolish as the words of any lover," he answered, and watched her thoughtfully as she made her way back to her father's side.

It was fear, not love, that held her in thrall, however, when, early the next morning, they made their way past the garishly clad Papal guards for their audience with the Pope. She had confided her intention to Céline the previous night as they sat at the window of their hotel room and watched the moon rise, full and bright over the roofs of the ancient city, and now the elder girl squeezed her hand and nodded reassuringly.

The chapel to which the pilgrims were escorted gleamed

gold and silver, a brilliant setting for the ladies in their black gowns and lace mantillas. Everybody, Thérèse thought, looked tall and distinguished, and there were so many splendidly robed officials that her heart sank. After two Masses had been offered those granted audience were to file past the Pope, kissing his shoe and his ring. That would be her opportunity to put her case before him. It had seemed so simple when she and Céline had sat together talking about it, but now that she was actually here the whole idea seemed impossible. It might be such a gross infringement of etiquette that she would be put in prison or excommunicated!

The long services were over and the tall, hawkfaced Pontiff was being escorted to a high backed chair, ringed about by officials. Thérèse, with the other ladies, began to shuffle forward in the long line. The gentlemen would be received later.

He was old, she thought, craning her neck, with piercing eyes, but he sat as straight as a ramrod, and his voice had been as sonorous as a young man's. His was a tremendous responsibility. The weight of Christ's Church rested on his shoulders and she had actually dared to imagine that she could persuade him to take an interest in her own small affairs!

Without knowing how she got there Thérèse found herself on her knees, her nose banging against the Pope's extended shoe. She straightened up, aware of a confusion of brilliant colours, and the long, age-veined, elegant hand of the white robed figure. Her heart was beating so fast that it seemed to drum in her ears, but she drew a deep breath and opened her mouth.

From the side Monsignor Révérony said in a low voice, "It is absolutely forbidden to speak to His Holiness."

Her courage was draining out of her as swiftly as the

memory of a dream. Then Céline's voice, urgent and husky, reached her from behind.

"Speak out."

She heard her own voice babbling.

"Most Holy Father, I have a great favour to ask of you. Most Holy Father, in honour of your jubilee, please let me enter Carmel at fifteen."

The Pope was frowning at her in bewilderment. Then his eyes shifted to Monsignor Révérony and he said, in slow careful French, "I do not quite understand."

"Your Holiness, this child is anxious to enter Carmel at fifteen," Monsignor Révérony said. "Her superiors are looking into the matter at this moment."

"Then do as your superiors tell you, my child," the Pope said, his gaze returning to Thérèse.

"Yes, but if you would only say the word, Most Holy Father, everybody would agree," she said, her courage returning with a rush.

"All's well, all's well," the Pope said, his eyes still piercing her through. "If God wants you to enter, then you will."

"But——" She opened her mouth to plead further but two of the Papal guards were hoisting her to her feet and hustling her away. She tried to twist her head around and saw him for one brief glimpse, his long hand raised in blessing, his eyes still fixed upon her.

She had made her attempt and bungled it. The Pope had been very kind, but he probably thought that she was an hysterical schoolgirl. The sense of failure was so crushing that she leaned against the nearest pillar and wept silently.

"My dearest child, you did your best," Louis was saying. "You spoke out bravely. So did Céline."

"I asked him for a special blessing upon Carmel," Céline said. "I didn't want you to be the only one to get into trouble for speaking out of turn."

Monsignor Révérony, to her relief, tactfully ignored her woebegone face when they started back for breakfast at the hotel.

Louis showed his distress openly. The thought that his precious daughter should have had all her plans shattered at the height of their trip was the cruellest mischance he could have imagined. He could bear disappointment for himself, but not for her.

To his surprise Thérèse had dried her eyes before the morning was over and seemed to have accepted the blow with an almost fatalistic calm.

When they left Rome the next morning she seemed to have thrown off her disappointment and apart from a faint redness about her eyelids, looked cheerful and pretty. They were to travel to Naples and thence to Assisi. Imperceptibly Louis's own distress began to lessen as Thérèse pointed out the beauties of the countryside from the window of the train and clung to his coat tails in half-pretended fright when the volcano of Vesuvius rumbled threateningly.

Assisi was a delight. She loved the winding streets and the ivy twined cloisters and the little church where St Francis had made the first Christmas Crib. Indeed she spent so long in the Convent of St Clare that, when she finally came out, it was to find herself alone with the last of the tourist coaches vanishing down the street. For a moment she stood irresolute, wondering how long it would be before her absence was noticed.

"Miss Thérèse, come and share my conveyance!" Monsignor Révérony called, appearing round a corner as promptly as if she had rubbed a lamp.

"I don't wish to turn anyone else out," she began nervously.

"Nonsense! You're so little that we can easily squeeze

you in," he said heartily.

Blushing hotly, she climbed up and found herself wedged between two solemn young priests who tried to make room for her as the coach set off after the others.

"Well, we are now on the homeward journey," Monsignor Révérony said, leaning forward to talk to her. "We go to France and then on to Genoa. You will be home in time for Christmas."

"Yes." She answered softly, the comfort and warmth of Les Buissonets filling her mind.

"You are fond of your home?" he questioned.

"Oh, it's a lovely house!" she said, her eyes kindling with pleasure. "I have lived there since I was four years old. It holds so many happy memories for me."

"And yet you are chafing at the bit to leave it," he observed. "When you enter Carmel you'll never see your home again, you know. And there will be no more jaunts to foreign parts, unless you are chosen for one of the missions."

"That would be marvellous!" she cried, clasping her hands tightly together. "I always wanted to be a missionary, when I wasn't wanting to be a hermit! But it won't matter if I never leave the enclosure at Lisieux for I shall carry the whole world within me, you see. I shall remember all this with such pleasure. Such great pleasure! But at Carmel I will have unimaginable vistas."

The coach rattled on and stopped. Climbing down, Thérèse bobbed a curtsey as Monsignor Révérony stepped into the road.

"It was very kind of you to let me share your carriage," she said politely. "I'm afraid I'm proving a sad nuisance to you all."

"Your conduct has been somewhat unusual," he conceded wryly. "I dread to think what His Lordship will say when he hears the news of your little escapade in Rome. You realize that I am bound to report it to him?"

"And it will tip the scales? Yes, Monsignor, I know that."

"You don't appear unduly concerned," he remarked. "Perhaps it was just a whim on your part."

"Oh, no." She looked up at him. "I still want to enter Carmel at the earliest possible moment. Believe me, but I hoped for so much from my visit to Rome. I really imagined that I had only to ask and the Pope would wave a magic wand and fly me on a magic carpet to Carmel. That was foolishness and self-loving too. I have always wanted my own way, you know, though I generally try to convince myself that God wants it too."

"And what does God want now, young lady?" he enquired.

"He is sleeping," she replied. "The Holy Child must sleep you see, and sometimes He leaves His toys scattered about as children do, until He wakes up and decides to play with them again."

"So! And what do the toys do if He flings them away?" he asked.

"Oh, they go on singing in their hearts, Monsignor," she said.

"Even when they are cruelly disappointed, with no hope of having their own will?"

"Even when they are flung into the dustbin," Thérèse said calmly. "Will you excuse me now? Papa will be certain I've been abducted or fallen into a river or something. He is apt to fret about me."

"Yes, of course. Run along, little one."

Thoughtfully, he watched her out of sight. Then he went inside to add another paragraph to the report he was compiling for the Bishop.

TEN

"So, the Bishop finally gave his consent!"

Uncle Isidore shook his head, laughing a little as he contemplated his niece's daring.

"Monsignor Révérony gave an excellent report of Thérèse's character and conduct," Louis said.

"And so we finally lose you." Isidore's eyes rested on Thérèse with affectionate regret.

"I am not going to vanish," she said, smiling back at him. "You will be able to come to the parlour on Wednesdays."

"It won't be the same," Cousin Jeanne said, "and you'll even miss my wedding, Thérèse! Oh, you would have made such a lovely bridesmaid."

"Céline and Marie will do the job beautifully," Aunt Elisa said. "Do cheer up! Anyone would think that Thérèse was going to be executed, instead of going to the one place she desires."

She spoke briskly, belying her sentiments by constantly dabbing her eyes.

"I wish you could all be as happy as I am," Thérèse said, looking round the handsomely appointed table.

This was her betrothal party, the last time she would visit her uncle's house. It had been a day of last events. She had gone to the Abbey to say goodbye to the teachers, and then to Madame Papinau who had wept a great deal and given her some gingerbread.

Now her entire family was gathered about the table.

Her eyes rested on each one in turn. Uncle Isidore and Aunt Elisa were reconciled, albeit reluctantly, to the idea of her becoming a nun. She wondered why she had ever found Uncle Isidore alarming. In the three months since the Bishop had given his consent he had been gentle and thoughtful, hiding his own misgivings far more successfully than her aunt concealed her tears. Cousin Marie had cried a great deal too, which was only to be expected, and Cousin Jeanne, who sat next to her fiancé and constantly touched his hand, looked at her as if she were some strange alien being whose behaviour was foreign to normal human contact.

Thérèse's eyes rested on Léonie. She had come back from the Visitation Convent more pale and tearful than ever. Only that morning she had said, "You skip towards Carmel as if you were going on a picnic! You have no idea of the deprivations and sacrifices you will meet. I could not endure them, and I am twenty-five. How will you at fifteen, contrive?"

"With difficulty," Thérèse said, laughing, but Léonie had refused to be consoled, and sat now, picking at the food before her and looking utterly downcast.

In contrast Céline was being very gay and lively, chattering and joking. She looked animated with a high colour and bright eyes, and Thérèse would have died rather than reveal that she had listened all night long to her muffled weeping.

Her eyes moved to Louis who was drinking his coffee and listening to the general conversation going on around him. Dear Papa! He had never uttered one word of complaint about the determination with which she had pursued her aim, but she knew how deeply he felt the imminent parting.

The next morning she was awake at dawn. A chill, grey

dawn but with the promise of sunshine to come. She was up and dressed before Céline was stirring, and risked vanity by glancing at herself in the mirror. With her hair tied back under a white kerchief, black dress and short cape, she looked, she thought, like a real postulant. Softly she tiptoed upstairs. Here, unnaturally tidy, was the beloved attic refuge which she had given to Céline for her own use. The caged birds greeted her as she removed the cover from the bars. Soon she too would enter a kind of prison so that her spirit could be freed.

She took a last look round and ran lightly down the stairs again to where her father was already waiting for her in the parlour. He said nothing but drew her towards him, kissing her forehead and gazing down at her with a question in his eyes. She answered him with a smile and he nodded as if some last doubt had been settled in his mind, and released her abruptly.

Thérèse went to the kitchen where Victoire was weeping into her apron and declaring in the same breath that it was the happiest day of her life.

"I always knew you were different from the rest, Miss Thérèse. You recall how you used to make little altars and beg two stubs of candle from me for the lighting of them? You'll not forget your old Victoire, will you?"

"Of course I won't!" Thérèse hugged her fiercely.

"Princess, it's time we were leaving."

Her father's quiet voice interrupted them. Thérèse planted a last kiss on the maid's tearstained cheek and turned, taking her father's hand and walking with him for the last time round the garden. The doves were already cooing and the daffodils nodded yellow trumpets above the young roses.

The walk to church was a silent one. Léonie's face was buried in her handkerchief and Céline's cheerful front had dissolved into tears. The rest of the family waited at the church door and they all went in together. The church was packed. Thérèse found herself nodding and smiling at people whom she knew only by sight. Even Madame Papinau was there, wrapped round in a faded gentility.

All through the Mass Thérèse was conscious of little things. She could hear Léonie's and Céline's sobbing, the little sniffs that Aunt Elisa kept giving, the way in which Uncle Isidore's voice kept breaking all through the responses.

The service over there was an expectant hush and then the sound of the grille being raised. The Mother Prioress, heavily veiled, stepped to the threshold and raised one arm in a beckoning gesture.

This was the moment of entry. She turned to be lost in a sea of embraces and then, her heart pounding, her legs shaking, took the short walk past the altar and entered the enclosure.

The grille clanged behind her like death and she was in gloom, a group of veiled figures facing her. From the grille behind Father Delatroette's voice sounded, low and contemptuous.

"Well, Mother Prioress, you may sing your Te Deum now, for you have your fifteen year old. If the bringing of a child into Carmel turns out badly, you have only yourself to blame, so you may take all the responsibility."

Ungracious words from a man whose authority had been thwarted. Poor Father Delatroette was certainly unable to hide his annoyance.

"My dear child!" The Prioress was embracing her warmly, drawing the sting of the priest's words.

The other nuns were throwing back their veils and embracing her. Introductions floated above her head. Sister John of the Cross. Sister Teresa of St Augustine. Sister

Marie Ange. Sister Agnes of Jesus who was her own dear Pauline. Sister Marie of the Sacred Heart who was her own Marie.

"I am Sister Marie of the Angels." A middle-aged nun with dreamy eyes was embracing her. "I am your novice mistress. Come with me to Mother Génevieve now. She is waiting to meet you."

Mother Génevieve was already a legend. Now in her eighties, it was she who had founded the Lisieux Carmel and been its first Prioress, and it was whispered in the town that she was a saint.

The old lady was propped up in bed in a tiny room leading off the choir. Her face was a network of fine lines, but her eyes were young and her voice unexpectedly strong as she said,

"You are to be known as Sister Thérèse of the Child Jesus and the Holy Face. Bear the name with joy.

It was the very name she would have chosen for herself. Thérèse could not resist beaming happily.

"I will show you the convent while the Sisters make their examination of conscience and then we will go to breakfast," Sister Marie of the Angels said.

Everything about the place delighted her, though she could not help noticing that it was very cold.

"We have a fire in the recreation room from November until February," the Novice Mistress said. "We do not have chairs or stools but sit on our heels or kneel if our limbs become cramped. This is your cell, but you must always remember that it does not belong to you. We own everything in common."

The tiny room with its own barred window sparkled with cleanliness. Thérèse looked round with pleasure at the narrow bed, the writing desk and bench, the basin and jug on the stone floor. On the wall, beneath a plain cross, a notice read,

'Daughter, what are you doing here?'

"We rise at five thirty in summer and at six thirty in winter," Sister Marie of the Angels was continuing. "You will rise at the first summons and repeat the morning Offering. Then you will wash, dress, tidy your cell, and come down to Mass. We will go to breakfast now."

The refectory was across a yard. As she entered Thérèse was conscious of the silence that reigned up and down the long tables. On the wall an empty-eyed skull gazed down. She sat at the end of the bench where the Novice Mistress indicated and looked at the meal before her. A slice of dry bread and a mug of warm water in which a few grains of sugar floated met her eyes. The signal to eat had been given for the nuns, with one accord, threw back their sleeves, pinned the end of the white napkin before them to their habits and began to eat.

"The Mother Prioress always likes to talk to the new postulants," Sister Marie of the Angels said, coming up to her as the nuns filed silently out. "Then our Chaplain, Father Youf, will instruct you for an hour. You understand that you will not be permitted to speak to the professed nuns or to the novices, unless you receive my permission before each occasion. Mother Génevieve, however, sees everyone for a few minutes each day. Come, we'll go to Mother Prioress now."

At close quarters Mother Marie Gonsague was taller than Thérèse had realized, her eyes sharper, with something in their expression that obscurely troubled the girl. She put her arm about Thérèse, hugging her with an ardour that had something hungry about it, exclaiming,

"What a sweet little postulant you make! We are so happy to have you with us, sweetheart. Now, if anything troubles you or displeases you, be sure to come and tell me all about it! I am always ready to hear the postulants' little complaints, and we shall be quite private, I assure you."

Her smile was so kindly that for an instant something in Thérèse surged up to answer it. It was gone in an instant and she raised troubled eyes to the avid face above her, saying,

"But I am not here to complain to you, Mother Prioress."

"So you think you will sail through your postulancy without begging for my help, do you?" The Prioress moved away and there was amusement in her voice. "Oh, you will not find it so easy, I assure you. There are those who have tried, but they come to me in the end. Poor little doves, their plumage all ruffled up, and I smooth them down so gently that they are forever grateful. Even nuns have affections, you know."

"To be directed towards God," Thérèse said.

"Of course, and we show our love for the Divine by caring for His fellow creatures," the Prioress said. "Now you are very young, quite a baby. There must be some little privilege you would enjoy?"

"Nothing, Mother Prioress," Thérèse said in bewilderment.

"Because you have only to ask," the Prioress continued. "Yes, Sister Marie of the Angels, what is it?"

Her voice had changed, crackling with irritation.

"Father Youf is here, Mother Prioress," the Novice Mistress said, standing impassive in the doorway.

"Very well, very well. Take her away then." Mother Marie Gonsague went over to the window and stood staring out into the cloisters.

"Come along, Sister." The Novice Mistress beckoned Thérèse out.

As they went down the corridor she said, her voice low, her face averted, "Mother Prioress is sometimes not very well. If you are troubled or need advice it would be better to come to me. You understand?"

"Yes, Sister." Thérèse hesitated, then ventured, "In Carmel human affections must be detached and the heart turned to God."

"You are a wise child," Sister Marie of the Angels said, glancing at her. "Mother Prioress is, of course, the Christ of our Community, and it is our duty to protect her at all times. Now you must meet Father Youf."

The interview was less alarming than she had expected. The chaplain was a rotund little man with twinkling eyes, who chatted to her pleasantly, asked kindly after her family, and ended by telling her to be a good girl and do her duty.

After that, seated next to a sullen faced girl in the same postulant dress as herself, she listened intently to Sister Marie of the Angels.

"The life of Carmel is the hidden life of Nazareth. We enter, not to escape from the world, but in order that we may concentrate on becoming channels of God's grace through our prayers and sacrifices. The discipline here is hard and the life one of constant mortification. As postulants you are free to leave at any time. Our doors are locked on the inside. Always remember that we come in here with the intention of submerging our will in the Will of the Divine. We have three rules—Poverty, Chastity and Obedience, and as postulants you will begin to practise those three virtues. Utter, implicit obedience to one's superiors, chastity of action and thought, a complete detachment from the worldly concerns. Those are the principles upon which our lives are built."

She paused, smiling at them.

"We begin with silence. At all times, except during our two half hour recreation periods each day, we keep silent unless it is absolutely necessary. At recreation we pause when the bell for silence is rung, even if it means stopping in the middle of a word. Now we will join the others for recreation before dinner."

As they went into the recreation room the other postulant tugged at Thérèse's sleeve.

"Is it true that you have two sisters here already?" she asked.

"Over there, by the window." Thérèse glanced longingly towards Sister Agnes and Sister Marie.

"I don't have any family," the other said. "I was brought up in orphanages. I'm Sister Martha of Jesus."

"Oh, but you have a family now," Thérèse said quickly. "We are all your sisters here. Come and tell me about yourself. What do you like to do best?"

"I don't do anything well," Sister Martha said resentfully. "They told me that I'm to help out in the kitchens and laundry. At recreation we can go and talk to the professed nuns, you know, so I won't mind if you go off and talk to your real sisters. I'm used to my own company."

"Then you will have to learn to get used to mine," Thérèse said, trampling her own longing ruthlessly underfoot. "Tell me what you have to do in the kitchens. Our maid, Victoire, used to let me help sometimes to bake cakes for Papa."

"How nice to have a maid," the other said sarcastically. "In the orphanage we were the maids and we seldom got cakes."

It was a relief when the bell rang and they filed across the yard again to the refectory.

A dish of cooked beans sprinkled with cheese, a mug of water and an apple faced her. Thérèse closed her eyes, fighting back nausea. Even the smell of beans made her feel sick, and the taste of them was unbearable. But they were there, evil and green, sneering under their coating of cheese.

She took a deep breath, swallowed, and began to eat.

Half an hour later, having vomited her meal into a hedge in the inner garden, she straightened up dizzily, wiping sweat from her brow.

"Sister Thérèse, have you nothing more useful to do than stand about daydreaming?" an elderly nun demanded, striding towards her.

"I've not been told, Sister," Thérèse began.

"Then use your initiative, girl. Pull up some of those weeds and don't stand gazing at them!"

"Yes, Sister." She bent to the task while the other strode off, muttering audibly that she'd always said it was a mistake to have children in Carmel.

"Sister Thérèse, what are you doing? I don't recall telling you to do any gardening," Sister Marie of the Angels exclaimed. "You are to go and help Sister Martha of Jesus in the laundry at once."

"Yes, Sister." Thérèse began to hurry towards the big, stone built laundry.

"Don't run, child. A good Carmelite doesn't run."

"No, Sister." Thérèse slowed down to a walk and entered the steaming laundry where three or four laysisters were beating dirt out of the wet linen with wooden paddles.

"If you saunter around like that, you'll never do much of value," one of them remarked. "Put this apron on and do a little work."

The paddles were heavy and made her wrists ache, but even more unpleasant were the sprays of cold, muddied water thrown up into her face by Sister Martha who looked as if she were taking out her ill humour on the habits. The temptation to glare at her was almost overwhelming, but if she did then poor Sister Martha would feel terribly guilty. On the other hand there was no way to endure cold, dirty water flung into her face. Instead she would pretend that she was being showered with cool, perfumed water. She smiled, banging the paddles rhythmically as the cold, dirty water trickled down her face.

"Child, go and wash your face and make yourself tidy. It will be recreation soon and then supper."

The Novice Mistress was chivvying them along like a worried hen with a flock of unruly chicks.

In her cell Thérèse looked in dismay at the shattered jug on the floor. Evidently someone had come in to borrow it and dropped it.

"Sister Thérèse! How very careless of you!" Sister Marie of the Angels had returned and was looking in consternation at the mess. "Kiss the floor at once and then collect all the pieces."

Long ago Zélie had tried to bribe her to kiss the floor and she had proudly refused. Now she was being told to kiss the floor for something she hadn't done. Indignation bubbled up in her. Sister Marie of the Angels would understand if she explained—and then someone else would get into trouble. Slowly, her face scarlet, she prostrated herself, pressing her lips against the icy stone.

After recreation there would be Benediction and then supper. She was already feeling tired and her head was aching. For a moment she was strongly tempted to burst into tears, but if she did they might begin to regret the decision to admit her at so young an age. She rose, the broken bits of the jug in her hand, and smiled.

At the evening recreation there was singing and several of the nuns had needlework or knitting with them. Thérèse allowed herself a few minutes precious conversation with Sister Agnes and Sister Marie and then went over to help one of the novices to wind some wool. The bell for Benediction ended the half hour and she went eagerly to her place behind the grille, only to find herself nodding off to sleep before the blessing had been given.

Supper was more palatable than the midday meal had been, with a plump kipper and spring greens and a pear tart with cream. Thérèse found herself eating heartily.

"Sister Thérèse, if you please!" The Prioress was rapping the table with her little gavel.

"Mother?" Thérèse hastily unpinned her napkin and stood up.

"Your examination of conscience, please," the Prioress said. "You have prepared it as I instructed?"

A little storm of anger rippled through her, but she kept her gaze lowered.

"You may examine your conscience privately before me, if you are too shy to speak out before your sisters," the Prioress said.

Her voice was suddenly kind, her eyes brilliantly compelling. There was an imperceptible stir among the nuns, a tension communicated in some indefinable way. The Novice Mistress had half risen, her face very still.

"I will accuse myself before my sisters," Thérèse said.

"Very well. Begin." The brilliant eyes were lowered.

"I accuse myself of unworthy resentment against the Father Superior after the words he spoke at my entry," she began nervously. "I accuse myself of seeking the company of my natural sisters. I accuse myself of spiritual pride."

"Has anyone in charity, anything else to say?"

"In charity I accuse Sister Thérèse of pulling up weeds without permission and of carelessness in breaking a jug," the Novice Mistress said.

"Not a very good beginning, child," the Prioress commented. "As your penance you may pick up all the litter you find until further notice."

"Yes, Mother Prioress." She took her seat again, wondering if it was permissible to dig a little hole and sink into it.

Twilight had fallen and she was waiting to receive her lamp and the blessing of the Novice Mistress. Sister Marie of the Angels smiled at her warmly, her dreaming eyes kind.

From behind the half-open door of the Prioress' cell came a ripple of laughter and a low, teasing voice, "Another bonbon, Sister Martha? We must leave a couple in the box in case little Thérèse looks in."

The lamp swayed in her hand as she clung to the stair rail, forcing herself to turn away from the light and the promise of human affection and make her way to the cell where the notice asked,

'Daughter, what are you doing here?'

'Trying to be a good postulant,' Thérèse answered in her mind. 'And oh, I have such a long way to go!'

ELEVEN

In the parlour Céline sat weeping, her face a dismal contrast to her summery dress and hat.

"One simply doesn't know what to do for the best! Uncle Isidore declares I am too young for the responsibility, but I am sure that Victoire and I will be able to manage. And Léonie is being quite splendid. She comes over from uncle's house every day and spends hours with Papa."

"What does the doctor say?" Sister Agnes spoke in a carefully controlled voice.

"He says it is cerebral palsy. Some sort of pressure on the cranial nerves which causes paralysis and mental confusion. There are days when he is quite his old self, you know, and there is always the possibility of what they call a spontaneous remission."

"Then we mustn't lose hope," Sister Marie said.

"By no means. Papa himself is hopeful of recovery. He has such a strong faith that everything is for the best."

"Papa is right," Thérèse said.

"How can you think such a thing?" Céline reproached. "This is a terrible affliction to be visited on him. Such a good, kind man to be struck down!"

"God won't send more than we can bear," Thérèse said.

"Well I hope you're right." Céline threw her a faintly irritated glance.

"Thérèse is always hopeful," Sister Agnes said. "But it will mean delaying her Clothing, unless Uncle Isidore stands in for Papa."

"The heat seems to aggravate the complaint," Céline said. "I think it would be wise to postpone the ceremony until winter."

"Thérèse will be sixteen in January," Sister Marie reminded them. "We could make it a double celebration."

"That would be lovely," Thérèse beamed. "There might even be snow. I've always loved snow!"

"You always had peculiar tastes," Céline said, laughing despite herself.

"Let it be January then," Sister Agnes said. "I will see Mother Prioress about it."

The sand in the hour glass had trickled its last, and they rose to shutter the grille.

Thérèse blew a kiss to her sister and went out with a light step.

In the corridor she paused for a moment, tasting the bitterness of disappointment. She had set her heart on a summer Clothing and now she must wait in the postulancy, a half and half nun, until Papa was well enough to give her away. Kind as Uncle Isidore was, it was unthinkable that he should take Papa's place. This cerebral palsy must be a terrible thing. In a way it was worse to be in Carmel hearing about it than to be at Les Buissonets witnessing it.

She could look back now and see so much more clearly little incidents they had not noticed at the time. Her father's moods of depression and irritability, his slow, slightly unsteady gait, his occasional hesitations of speech —they had all been symptoms of his approaching illness. She blamed herself bitterly for having been so wrapped up in her own concerns.

"Sister Peter is waiting to be taken to the refectory," Sister Marie of the Angels said, coming round the corner.

"I'm just going, Sister."

Thérèse stifled a sigh. Everyone had a cross to bear and

hers was the grumbling, invalid old nun who insisted in taking a full part in the activities of the Community though she ought, by rights, to have been in the infirmary waiting placidly for death.

Sister Peter was in choir, in the chair which she claimed as her own even to the extent of tying a bit of string round its leg so that nobody else could use it. Thérèse knelt, crossed herself swiftly, and then stood, hands clasped before her, waiting until Sister Peter deigned to notice her presence.

"You've kept me waiting for long enough," she said at last. "We shall both be late and you know how I hate to be rushed."

"I won't rush you, Sister Peter. We can make it in time without hurrying if we start now," Thérèse said.

"Let me get my breath then." Sister Peter closed her eyes and, with a look of suffering martyrdom on her face, allowed Thérèse to haul her to her feet where she swayed dangerously like an overloaded battleship. In her youth she had been a powerfully built woman. Now she was like a hoary old oak, threatened by wind and storm, its roots twisted and fading, but still clinging tenaciously to life.

"Not so fast, girl! You'll have me on my face if you gallop along like a racehorse!" she complained.

"I'm sorry, Sister Peter." Thérèse slowed her footsteps.

Darkness was falling already as if to remind them that summer would soon be over. A cold breeze had sprung up, ruffling the ends of Thérèse's short veil, and a few leaves drifted down from the chestnut tree in the corner.

"Fifty years I've been enclosed and you must be the slowest postulant I've ever had the misfortune to endure," Sister Peter said crossly. "My supper will be quite cold by the time we get there."

"We'll go a little faster then, Sister." Thérèse obediently

hurried up again.

Somewhere in her head a tune had begun to play, a lilting waltz such as she had heard at dancing class, but not thumped out on a piano. An orchestra swelled out and the darkening chilly yard was a ballroom decorated in white and gold round which gaily dressed couples whirled, the men handsome in their evening suits, the girls in deliciously frilled pastel gowns with jewels sparkling on necks and arms. For a moment only the scene lasted and then it was gone and the music was gone, and there was only the yard and Sister Peter's harsh old voice.

"Do get a move on! What are you dreaming about?"

Fifty years, Thérèse thought. Fifty years was a very long time. Sister Peter must have been young and lovely once, and now she was old and sick and perhaps some of her bad temper sprang from fear because her death was so near and her youth all gone.

"It is such a privilege to be here, Sister," Thérèse said. "I wouldn't be anywhere else in the world!"

"Well, right now I want to be in the refectory, eating my supper," Sister Peter said, lurching forward again and coming down on Thérèse's foot.

"Here we go then, Sister. Gently now." Carefully she piloted the old woman into the refectory, settled her at her place and cut up her bread into small pieces.

"Thank you, Sister Peter." Thérèse bowed her head, smiling.

The Prioress rapped her gavel smartly and Thérèse moved at once to the centre of the room, raising her voice in the silence.

"I accuse myself of being late for supper and of being the cause of Sister Peter's also being late for supper."

"For your penance kiss the feet of your sisters and beg your food for a week," the Prioress said.

There was a little ripple of indignation from the table where Sister Agnes and Sister Marie sat among the professed nuns. The penance was a severe one for a postulant, but Mother Marie de Gonsague was always harsh with Thérèse.

"Thank you, Mother Prioress." Thérèse smiled again even more brilliantly and prostrated herself.

"She is too hard on her!" Sister Agnes said to the Novice Mistress. "I cannot understand it. She was so eager for her to be admitted, and now she goes out of her way to find fault with her."

"Thérèse is not what she expected. She is not what any of us expected," Sister Marie of the Angels said. "I wish Thérèse would confide more in me. I can't criticize the way in which she carries out her work, nor the fervour with which she observes her religious duties, but she never confides the state of her soul to me."

"I can't help you," Sister Agnes said. "She seldom talks to us either, even when it is allowed at recreation. She prefers to spend her time with Sister Martha of Jesus who must be the most unsuitable candidate we've ever had! God forgive me, but it annoys me to even see the wretched girl."

"If it were my decision I would send her away," Sister Marie of the Angels said, "but she is a favourite of the Mother Prioress."

"Yes." Sister Agnes nodded in silence, charity binding her tongue.

In her cell Thérèse knelt, wrestling with herself. She knew what she had to do because her conscience had instructed her that she was the only one who could undertake the task, but her heart failed her. It was more than probable that she would be sent away for her presumption, but she had to speak out. To close one's eyes to evil was to condone it.

At last, outwardly calm but inwardly quaking, she rose and went along to Sister Martha's cell.

"Sister, may I speak with you?" She hesitated at the door.

"Yes, of course." The other looked up with a welcoming smile quite different from her usual frown.

'In a few minutes she will be throwing me out of her cell', Thérèse thought.

Aloud she said, her voice shaking a little, "It is about Mother Prioress. You are very fond of her."

"She is a wonderful person," Sister Martha said defensively.

"Indeed she is and it's our duty to love her because she is the Christ in our Community," Thérèse said. "But your affection for her is a—a very passionate one. The other Sisters will not speak of it to you because they are more strictly bound by their vows, but I haven't made any vows yet, and I can talk to you as an ordinary girl. You love Mother Marie de Gonsague in a way that—in the world it would be frowned upon, but in here it becomes a kind of poison."

"I've done nothing wrong!" Sister Martha had coloured up. "There's no harm in natural affection."

"Between two women a natural affection can so easily become an unnatural one when sensuality creeps in." Thérèse said. "We would probably be married and have babies but we have chosen to mortify our fleshly desires, and if we come in here and seek to feed them we cheat ourselves and God. It would be much better for us to remain in the world and make a happy marriage than to come in here and lose our souls."

"Have you never craved a little human warmth sometimes?" Sister Martha asked, beginning to cry.

"All the time," Thérèse said. "I was reared in a family where we were always hugging and kissing, but one cannot indulge in such behaviour in a convent. It would cause great scandal if it became known, and if it were to remain hidden it would still poison the very feelings we think so precious. Don't you see?"

"Yes, but it's hard!" Sister Martha wept again.

"Very hard," Thérèse said, and went out slowly.

Mother Marie de Gonsague, glancing up from the convent accounts, gave a slightly surprised smile when she beheld Thérèse.

"Where is Sister Martha?" she enquired. "She usually pays me a little visit at this time."

"Sister Martha won't be coming, Mother Prioress," Thérèse said.

"Is she sick?" The Prioress half rose.

"No, Mother, but she won't be coming."

Thérèse had advanced into the room and stood, her brilliant blue eyes enormous in her small face.

"Sister, what exactly are you trying to say?" Mother Marie de Gonsague demanded.

There was a box of candied fruits open on the desk. Thérèse picked it up, closed the lid, and held it out wordlessly. Then she genuflected and went out.

"Sister Thérèse hasn't got a stomach ache, has she?" Sister Marie of the Angels enquired, coming in a few minutes later. "I met the dear child on the stairs just now and she looked quite ill. Perhaps we ought to allow some mitigation of the rules for her?"

"That child is stronger than any of us," the Prioress said. Her voice was faintly bitter, but she was smiling. "Don't be afraid of being too hard on her. She can bear more than you or I could imgaine!"

"Her poor father is very ill, I understand." The Novice

Mistress shook her head sadly. "I wonder if he had some premonition of it and if that had something to do with his supporting Thérèse's entry at so early an age."

"If he had not supported her she would have probably battered down the doors in order to get in," the Prioress said dryly.

A few days later Father Youf, his expression puzzled, looked intently at the little figure kneeling before him.

"I think you had better think again about that question," he said. "I wished to know your reason for entering Carmel."

"To become a saint, Father," she repeated.

"Like Teresa d'Avila, I suppose?"

"Oh, no, Father. Greater than she was," Thérèse said simply. "She had some very human faults, you know, even though she was such an important saint."

"And you haven't, I suppose?"

"Oh, I'm full of them," she said cheerfully. "Every morning, just for a second as I wake up, I'm as perfect as if God had just created me, and then as the day wears on I get less and less perfect, like a child learning to walk who keeps falling over and getting up again."

"But you weep over your faults?"

"No, Father. That would only make God feel unhappy," she said earnestly. "I tell Him jokes."

"Jokes?" Father Youf closed his eyes briefly.

"The silly little things that happen to make us smile," she explained. "I tell them to Him to make Him laugh a little. I don't think one has the right to go moaning to Him all the time."

"And you intend to become a great saint? You know about the four stages of prayer, the difference between interior and exterior vision, the stages of mystical contemplation, I suppose?"

144

"No, Father."

"Then your ambition is presumptuous," he said coldly. "Nobody sets out to become a saint. It is a grace conferred upon those who lead lives of heroic virtue or die as martyrs for the Faith. What will you do with yourself in Carmel?"

"Oh, I shall pray for souls, especially for priests," she said with a flash of mischief.

"And become a saint, I suppose? Your pride astounds me."

"I don't feel proud," she said in surprise. "Oh, sometimes I feel a little bit pleased with myself if I've kept my temper or done a bit of extra work, but that's not bad because any good I do is brought out in me by God. You don't call a rose proud because it has lovely petals, do you?"

"And how near are you to being a saint?"

"Right at the beginning," she said, "and that may be where I end up too, Father, and it may be the place where God wants me to be."

"That will be all, Sister." He blessed her rapidly and watched her leave.

The Novice Mistress, bringing him a cup of coffee, said, "The little Thérèse's father is said to have recovered slightly from his latest stroke. We are hoping he will be able to give her away at her Clothing ceremony. She is a good little soul. Don't you think so?"

"I think she is the glory of this Carmel," he said slowly, "but we must take very good care never to let her guess it."

The news of Louis's recovery spread like laughter through the convent. Léonie and Céline came to the parlour with word that he was convalescing.

"Slowly but surely," Léonie said, her eyes bright. "Dr Neele says he must have no excitement or worry. It's a strange thing, but whenever he feels an attack coming on he covers his head with a scarf or cloth or anything he can lay his hands on. Do you remember, Thérèse, when you were very little and saw Papa in the garden, his head muffled, and all the time he was somewhere else?"

"I didn't understand what it meant then," Thérèse said, "but it must have been a glimpse of what was to come."

But as the months passed, and Louis's improvement continued, the memory of that sinister childhood vision was overlaid with hope for the future.

She was to be Clothed a few days after her sixteenth birthday and no bride ever made more fervent preparations to receive her lover.

'For I am in love,' Thérèse thought. 'What I feel is what all girls feel, but I will never be disappointed in my affections. My lover will never die, or leave me, or lose interest in me as earthly husbands do.'

'And how do you know you're the chosen bride?' an insidious voice whispered. 'You're very young and very lovely. You could leave here and help Léonie and Céline to care for your father. You could have a real flesh and blood husband like Cousin Jeanne.'

"Oh Sister Marie, I've made such a mistake!" Tremblingly she faced the Novice Mistress.

"You've discovered that you have no vocation for the religious life," the other said.

"Sister, how did you know?" Her mouth fell open in surprise.

"Because we all feel exactly the same as you do before we make our vows," Sister Marie of the Angels said. "I am told that brides in the world have the same doubts and misgivings."

"But I am not worthy of my bridegroom," Thérèse said anxiously.

"Dear child, if our bridegroom had to wait until a worthy bride was found He would be lonely for ever," the Novice Mistress said affectionately. "Now go to bed and sleep well. Tomorrow is your betrothal day."

She had prayed for snow, but the sky was dappled with the promise of rain and there was a dampness in the air when she woke to the clapping of the castanets. She sprang out of bed, feeling as if she could have danced down to Mass.

The Ceremony of Clothing would be later in the morning when the Bishop had arrived, so there was breakfast first with a sliced peach laid at her place with the usual bread and water. She wondered where on earth they had obtained a fresh peach in the middle of January.

"Wait until you see your bouquet," Sister Agnes whispered as they were helping her to dress. "Hothouse lilies! Uncle Isidore had them sent round as a gift. Oh, Thérèse, you make a beautiful bride!"

She stood back clasping her hands, her eyes brimming with happy tears.

The church was crowded, but she had eyes only for her father. He had lost weight, she thought, and his white hair was receding but his eyes were serene, his smile both loving and proud, and only a faint tremor of his hand betrayed his recent illness.

"Princess, you look lovely!" He stood back and examined her, nodding his head. "Céline and Léonie chose the dress, you know, and the veil was fashioned from a length of lace that your dear mother made with her own hands."

The gown was of white velvet, high necked with long, narrow sleeves, its skirt swept round into a graceful bustle with a short train. Under the filmy veil her golden ringlets fell below her shoulders, and her bouquet of lilies was tied with a ribbon that matched her eyes.

Standing before the glittering altar, aware of the relatives and friends bunched up in the pews behind, she made her vows in a clear, firm voice, that echoed high and sweet through the church. Her father, gravely dignified, handed her over to the Bridegroom and the Bishop placed the gold ring upon her wedding finger. The choir, seeing but not seen behind the grille, began to sing the Te Deum. One of the assisting priests turned to whisper that Te Deums were sung only at final Professions, but His Lordship waved the objection aside.

Thérèse moved to the grille where the chaplain waited, his voice sibilant through the narrow bars.

"Thérèse of the Child Jesus and the Holy Face, do you of your own free will renounce the world with all its pleasures, and consecrate yourself as a bride of Christ to live in poverty, chastity and obedience, to embrace cold, privation, loneliness and silence unto death?"

"I do." Her voice rang out like a bell.

The heavy grille was raised. She stepped within and it clanged behind her. A long sigh ran through the congregation and then there was a long silence.

The bride had gone and in her place, flanked by white-robed nuns, walked a slim figure in brown habit and sandals, her head wrapped in a white toque, a black scapular and veil covering her shoulders and over it a white cloak, symbol of the novice. Prostrate, with arms extended, she lay in the centre of the aisle while Louis accepted the bag of white silk containing her long ringlets.

The choir sang again and she was led for the last time beneath the grille. There were nuns all about, giving her the kiss of peace. Even old Sister Peter was there, clasping Thérèse's hands in her own arthritic ones as she whispered, "Well done. God bless you, girl."

Alone she walked through the cloisters to the chapel

and knelt before the statue of the Christ child, laying her lilies at his feet, bowing her head as she uttered her own private dedication.

"Lord, let me be forgotten and trodden down like a grain of sand."

The prayer done, she raised her head, letting the joy of the day flood her being, and saw that the graceful little statue was covered with fine flakes of sparkling snow.

TWELVE

It was too cold to sleep. Sometimes Thérèse felt as if she would die with the damp, cold of the Norman winters in her bones, chapping her hands and feet and making her chest hurt when she tried to breathe deeply. There was a fire in the recreation room but she warmed herself at it only when her shivering became so uncontrollable that she feared the others might notice. Singularity was something she dreaded above all else. It was bad enough to be the youngest and the smallest without having her small sacrifices noted.

How strange to think that she was just twenty-one years old. She was a mature woman, though inside she felt no different from the eager fourteen year old who had begged the Pope to let her enter Carmel. No, that wasn't true. She had learned to control her feelings, to bite back the sharp retort, to smile even when she was so depressed that the world lay like a leaden weight on her shoulders.

She had even managed to smile, when, just a month after her Clothing, Uncle Isidore had come to tell them, gravely and kindly, that Louis had had another attack and, for his own sake, had been moved to the asylum. Céline visited him every week and sometimes came away in tears because he didn't recognize her at all but sat, wild eyed and twitching, muttering of his vocation for the religious life. There were periods when he was quite lucid and asked after the family, promising that as soon as he was well enough he would visit them.

It was harder for Céline than for any of them.

"I had planned to join you in Carmel," her sister had confessed. "Ever since we went to Rome I have cherished the wish to enter the religious life, but I was going to wait for a year or two so that Papa wouldn't feel he was losing all his daughters at once. Now there is still the chance of a permanent remission, and it would be dreadful if Papa was allowed to come home and found me already enclosed."

So Céline had sacrificed her own inclinations and waited patiently for the day when she too would pass beneath the grille. Céline was a heroine, Thérèse thought tenderly, to be ranked with her own favourite Joan of Arc.

In her own way Léonie was a heroine too. It was so clear that she had a vocation and so clear that she had not yet developed the strength of will necessary for perseverance. She had now returned to the Visitation Convent and they were all hoping against hope that this time she would settle down.

Thérèse's own final Profession had been delayed until four months before her eighteenth birthday.

"The Bishop and Father Delatroette both feel that you will still be very young to make your perpetual vows," the Prioress had said. "Extra time in the novitiate will benefit you enormously."

In fact she had never left the novitiate, for even when her white veil had been exchanged for the black one, Mother Marie de Gonsague had given a tight, triumphant little smile and said,

"You are still so very young, my dear child, that I am going to keep you among the novices for a year or two. Your work will be in the laundry."

If she had hoped for some reaction she had been disappointed. Thérèse had merely smiled tranquilly and genuflected.

The laundry work was backbreaking and unpleasant. Thérèse wasn't sure which she hated more—the freezing cold water in which everything had to be rubbed, squeezed and rinsed or the steaming hot room where the ironing was done. Her mornings, after Mass and the examination of conscience and breakfast, were spent over washtub and ironing board or carting baskets of wet clothes out into the yard to peg them on the lines. After recreation and the midday meal there was the refectory to be scrubbed and polished, the flower beds to weed, the day's meditation to be written up, Sister Peter to be hauled about from one place to the next, Vespers, another examination of conscience, Benediction, a second recreation at which sewing or knitting must be done, supper, and then the privacy of her bare little cell.

The only way to get through was to take each day as it came, to live each moment calmly with a smile, never to excuse oneself even if one was scolded unjustly, never to ask for favours, never to show hurt or pain or impatience. Above all, it had to be done unobtrusively, because when people noticed sacrifice it lost something as a rare perfume exposed to the air loses some of its fragrance.

Pulling the three grey blankets up to her chin and huddling into their meagre warmth, Thérèse wondered if it ever became any easier. She had a shrewd suspicion that it became even harder and that the more one tried to advance in the spiritual life the more one fell back. She had been inestimably fortunate in having as her model saintly old Mother Généviève. The few minutes she spent each day in her company were bright and warm. Thérèse never came away without a few kindly words of encouragement.

But Mother Généviève had been very old, so old that during the last months of her life she had fallen into a gentle dream, rambling about Mother Anne of Jesus who long ago had brought the first Carmelites to France.

"You must sit with her," the Prioress told Thérèse, "it will be edifying for you to keep vigil at a death bed."

It had not been edifying at all. Thérèse had knelt motionless for hours watching the shrunken figure and wrinkled face of the old woman, but she had felt nothing at all even when the great bell tolled her final passing.

Afterwards she had gone into the sacristy and gazed down at the white shrouded figure, hands folded, eyes closed. In the corner of one eye a tear still hung, and Thérèse had soaked it up with the corner of a small piece of linen. She carried with her dedication and a tiny copy of the Gospels in which she had pressed the white flower that Louis had given her long ago in the garden of Les Buissonets.

It was as if the death of old Mother Génévieve had opened the door for others. Within a month an epidemic of influenza had swept through the convent. Aching limbs, splitting headaches, hacking coughs and soaring temperatures had become the order of the day. Thérèse herself had caught the infection very lightly and been pressed into infirmary service.

Dr de Cornières found good use for Thérèse's services, for she was apparently tireless, trotting about obediently and not shrinking from the most unenviable tasks.

"I always know when you are coming, Sister," he remarked one day.

"Oh?" She glanced up at him.

He had been going to say that she brought with her a tranquillity that was like balm, but the worried little pucker between her brows made him fearful of embarrassing her.

"Your sandals squeak," he said, and was rewarded by

her delighted laughter.

She had woken early one morning with the conviction that something was wrong, and in going into Sister Madeline's cell had found her fellow nun lying, fully clad on her narrow bed, her eyes closed, her hands already folded as if she had tried to die as neatly and as perfectly as possible. To her own surprise Thérèse was not in the least nervous, but had fetched a wreath and a candle before going to inform the rest of the Community.

It had been a hard time, but she had found a physical and mental strength within herself she had not known. Even Father Delatroette had smiled at her kindly when he came to officiate at the Mass of Thanksgiving that marked the end of the epidemic.

Then it had been back to the laundry and its unremitting labour, back to being scolded for something or other every time she met Mother Marie Gonsague, of having to endure Céline's outbursts of heartbroken sobbing when she came to the parlour. Louis was no better and Céline herself was torn between her determination to live as mortified a life as possible and her desire to please Uncle Isidore by joining in various social activities.

"But you cannot possibly go to a ball!" Thérèse had exclaimed in horror.

"I cannot refuse. These are important friends of Uncle Isidore's."

"You made a vow of chastity," Thérèse said.

"Which I will keep. Honestly, Thérèse, you seem to think that I'm going to spend the evening in Sodom and Gomorrah, instead of a Catholic social dance," Céline exclaimed.

"You won't dance, will you?" Thérèse asked anxiously.

"I can't make a fool of myself by sitting like a dummy all evening. I have such a pretty new dress, and Uncle

Isidore has invited a very charming young man to escort me."

"You're betrothed to the Christ! How can you bear anyone else to even touch you?"

"Thérèse, you're being absolutely unreasonable!" Céline exploded. "It's all very well for you in here to preach good conduct to me, but I have to live in the world and have the right to a little pleasure now and then."

Deep down Thérèse knew that she was being unreasonable, that Céline deserved a little innocent fun, but she could not endure the thought of the brilliantly lighted ballroom and the spectre of Céline in her new gown dancing on the arm of some faceless, menacing figure who dipped and twirled, coat tails flying.

Kneeling before the altar, Thérèse sent forth her will as strongly as she could, building up Céline in her mind, not dancing, but standing still. She imagined it so strongly that she felt as if she could have reached out and touched her. The picture faded, and she began to cry though she had no idea why she should suddenly feel so miserable.

"And I didn't dance," Céline said. Her voice and her face were full of rueful amusement. "I was determined to stand up for every waltz, polka and quadrille, but I swear to you that when we reached our table my feet went as heavy as lead and I couldn't have moved a step. So I sat there all evening, stuffing myself with food, and refusing every dance until my poor escort wandered off and found himself a more obliging partner!"

"Did you mind very much?" Thérèse asked.

"Not really. He was a very dull young man," Céline assured her.

The question of Céline's social life faded into the background with the excitement of the election of the new Prioress. Thérèse had no vote in the Chapter, only two members of the same family being allowed to vote but she watched the proceedings anxiously. Mother Marie de Gonsague had hoped for re-election, but Sister Agnes had been nominated. She was young for such a position, but she was sensible and scrupulously fair with none of Mother Marie de Gonsague's harshness or her tendency to make favourites.

Sister Marie canvassed without shame for her younger sister and was even a little hurt when Thérèse held aloof.

"Anyone would think that you don't want her to win," she said reprovingly.

"I don't have a vote," Thérèse said, "so it doesn't much matter what I want. If Sister Agnes is the chosen one it will be because the Sisters want her, not because I have been running around extolling her virtues."

Sister Marie clicked her tongue, reflecting that Thérèse was sometimes very difficult to understand.

Sister Agnes was however elected, though by such a slender majority that some of the nuns joked that there ought to have been a recount.

"Now we shall have everything turned upside down," Sister Aimée of Jesus remarked audibly.

"New brooms have the right to sweep clean," Sister Marie retorted.

Mother Agnes, as she now was, speedily betrayed wisdom as well as energy when she made the new appointments. The finances of the convent needed straightening out, so Sister Marie was appointed as bursar. There were those who muttered about family favouritism but Sister Marie was quick at figures and soon brought the account books into some sort of order. Mother Marie of the Angels was made sub-prioress where her dreaminess and faulty memory wouldn't matter. The New Novice Mistress was Mother Marie de Gonsague, an announcement that raised eyebrows all round.

"Mother Marie de Gonsague cannot possibly be expected to deal with the novices all by herself," Mother Agnes said, ignoring the raised eyebrows. "I am therefore appointing Sister Thérèse of the Child Jesus as her assistant. I am also appointing Sister Thérèse as assistant in the sacristy."

Thérèse's face was a mixture of delight and consternation. To help in the sacristy was a privilege she had always secretly craved. It would give her inestimable joy to handle the sacred objects and to arrange flowers at the feet of the Christ Child, but the sacristan, Sister Teresa of St Augustine, set her teeth on edge. Thérèse couldn't understand what it was about the gentle, soft-voiced nun that irritated her so much. She would make every effort to overcome her dislike, Thérèse vowed, for it was unthinkable that she should go into the sacristy and harbour any resentment.

Mother Marie de Gonsague was a different kettle of fish. She had excellent qualities, Thérèse knew, but she could not imagine that the ex-Prioress would have anything but an unsettling influence on the novices. It would be left to herself to make peace, to wean the more easily led from adoration of Mother Marie's genuine impulses of kindness, to soften and interpret Mother Marie's harsher strictures. It was a task calling for the diplomacy of a Cardinal rather than the efforts of a girl of twenty, and her heart quailed at the prospect.

But at least it meant she no longer had to endure the icy water and steaming irons of the laundry. With a light step she went out into the garden.

"Is it true you are to be assistant Novice-Mistress?" a lively young postulant enquired, approaching her.

"I fear so." Thérèse gave the other a wry little smile.

Sister Marie of the Trinity was a slender, graceful girl, only a few months younger than herself. There was something about her that reminded Thérèse of Léonie. Sister

Marie of the Trinity had already spent two years at a Carmel in Paris and failed to settle down there, and this second attempt had not been viewed by either Father Delatroette or Father Youf with much favour.

"Congratulations!" she exclaimed now. "Oh, we were so pleased when we heard. Mother Marie de Gonsague terrifies me out of my wits. She is exactly like a wolf."

"Sister, that is no way to refer to your Novice Mistress," Thérèse said.

"Well, she is. We all say so!"

"None of you has any right to talk in such a fashion about Mother Marie Gonsague," Thérèse said, taking a deep breath and deciding that she might as well begin as she meant to go on.

"You are here to learn obedience, and obedience begins with respect for your superiors. If you don't wish to practise virtue in here you might as well return to the world and see if you get on any better out there!"

She stopped because Sister Marie of the Trinity had burst into tears.

"I'm sorry! I said I'm sorry," she moaned, tears spurting as freely as they had once gushed from the eyes of the child Thérèse.

"You spoke without due thought," Thérèse said, "and you'll not do it again. Don't cry, Sister. You seem to spend a lot of your time in weeping."

"I can't help it." Sister Marie of the Trinity stood, helplessly sobbing.

"Then you mustn't waste your tears," Thérèse said swiftly, bending to pick up one of the shells that bordered the neatly raked paths. "You must catch them in this shell. Quickly, Sister! There's one running down the side of your nose, and one falling off your chin. Quick!"

"Sister Thérèse, you're a fool!" Sister Marie of the

Trinity exclaimed and began to giggle helplessly, the tears drying up as she tried vainly to catch them in her shell.

"Some of them I catch by the scruff of the neck and others I catch by their wingtips," she confided to Mother Agnes. "They are such dear, good girls and they try so hard. I wish I didn't have to scold them."

"You have an excellent influence on them," Mother Agnes said. "They will confide in a girl of their own age, when they might feel a little awed by Mother Marie Gonsague. I have great faith in your judgement, child."

"I wish I had as much!" Thérèse exclaimed.

"You must have confidence in yourself," Mother Agnes said.

"No. I shall do my best and have confidence in God," Thérèse said with decision.

Her own confidence was often badly shaken in the months that followed, though she never allowed the novices to guess it. Her position was proving even more delicate than she had imagined it would be. Mother Marie de Gonsague was far too busy trying to court popularity to have time to spare for scolding, which meant that Thérèse had to restrain her natural gaiety and find fault when she would much have preferred to close her eyes to their little imperfections.

"You never give credit even for trying!" one of the novices flung at her some months later. "We do try, but you never even notice! Why, they forgot to serve me with any dessert today and I said nothing about it!"

"But now that you have drawn my attention to the matter I will speak to the Refectory Sister and you will come with me as soon as the recreation bell goes to reprove her thoughtlessness," Thérèse said.

"But that's not what I meant. I was simply pointing out——"

"That God gave you the chance to make a little sacrifice for Him and you were afraid it might go unremarked by human eyes. Now you have lost that opportunity and must tell the Refectory Sister of her carelessness, so that she has the chance to make amends."

"You're as hard as nails!" the other burst out. "What sacrifices do you ever make, I'd like to know!"

"You are right, Sister. I do so little that I want all of you to be better than I am," Thérèse said, beaming.

"She never does anything wrong," Sister Mary Magdalen complained. "I've never seen her looking miserable, or bad-tempered. I've never heard her ask for a favour, or even take advantage of the privileges she could have. She never even spends any time with her blood kin. She never makes excuses when she is accused at general confession. I watch her all the time, hoping she'll make a mistake, but she never does. I admire her enormously, but I don't like her. I don't like her at all."

"The Martin girl has a very easy time of it if you ask me," Sister Aimée grumbled, watching Thérèse walking in the garden. "As far as I can tell, she spends her mornings gossiping with the postulants and her afternoons strolling round the garden. And now there's talk of the other sister, Céline, joining us one day. I shall spare no efforts to prevent it, for we shall be overrun with Martins if we don't take care."

"Her poor father is very ill," one of the lay Sisters reminded her. "She never asks for extra time in the parlour when her sister comes. I never hear her complain."

"I should like to know what she has to complain about!" Sister Aimée said, so loudly that the figure walking tranquilly down the path must surely have heard.

Now, huddled under her blankets, Thérèse stifled an involuntary sob. She had always scorned cheap popularity and done everything in her power to cultivate detachment but it wasn't pleasant to be disliked and misunderstood. Some of her novices knew what she was trying to do, and showed their gratitude in little, touching gestures of affection, but many of them thought her cold and hard, well, she had not renounced the world in order to be loved by the world.

She punched her hard pillow, wincing as the coarse wool rasped her chilblained fingers, and tried to warm her toes by rubbing her feet together. Some of the Sisters inflicted real pain on themselves with hooked crosses that dug into the flesh and nettles tied to their scourges to raise blisters when they took the discipline but she had never had the courage to imitate them.

Her fingers groped for the bit of linen with which she had soaked up Mother Génévieve's tear. It was all she had to link her with the saintly old nun, for when her few bits and pieces had been shared out among the Community after her funeral Thérèse had been left out.

"I would have liked something of yours," she murmured, eyelashes drooping as she began to slide into an exhausted sleep.

It seemed to her that the first rays of dawn striking through the little barred window of her cell solidified into a veiled and shining figure, and Mother Génévieve's voice rang softly through the silence.

"Silly child, don't cry! Don't you know that I left you my heart?"

THIRTEEN

"So now we are all here together!" Mother Agnes of Jesus looked round at her three sisters with loving affection.

Sister Marie of the Sacred Heart had put on a little weight as she approached her mid-thirties but it suited her just as it suited Thérèse to be slender. The Prioress looked with particular affection at the third member of the trio. Dear Céline had been so patient and courageous during the years of Papa's illness. They had not grieved when he had died the previous summer for his last weeks had been a martyrdom and in the end he had babbled of monasteries and his desire to enter one, not remembering wife or daughters or anything of the years before.

Céline had arranged the funeral and gone to bring Léonie back from the Visitation Convent. On the very eve of her Profession she had changed her mind again. Uncle Isidore had taken her to live in his house, and Cousin Jeanne and her husband had moved into Les Buissonets.

There had been some anxious moments before Céline's admittance. It was unheard of to have four sisters in the same convent, and at times discussions about it threatened to become acrimonious. But even Sister Aimée had relented and, within a couple of months of Louis's death, Céline Martin had become Sister Généviève of St Teresa, and was now a novice under the direction of Mother Marie de Gonsague and Thérèse.

"I wish that Léonie were settled happily," Mother Agnes said, reverting to an earlier theme. "It frets me to think of her struggles. Life has always been so hard for the poor girl."

"Léonie will go back to the Visitation Convent after I am dead," Thérèse said, "and the next time she will take her final vows and become an excellent nun."

"Thérèse what a dreadful thing to say!" Sister Génévieve exclaimed.

"You don't feel ill, do you?" Sister Marie asked anxiously.

"I feel fine," Thérèse said cheerfully, "but I won't make old bones. You don't have to pull such long faces! What's so dreadful about going to Heaven?"

"I remember when you were small that you were forever hoping to kill off all the family," Sister Marie said.

"I used to think how lovely it would be if we could all die and fly up to Heaven together," Thérèse said. "Papa was doing some painting one day, up a ladder, and I can remember hanging onto the bottom of the ladder and hoping he'd fall off and squash me flat so we could both go to Heaven at the same moment."

"Mother Agnes, you ought to get Thérèse to write down all these childhood tales!" Sister Marie exclaimed. "Why, she might die young as she threatens and then they'd all be lost."

"Everyone has childhood tales to tell," Mother Agnes said doubtfully.

"But not everyone managed to get into Carmel at fifteen," Sister Génévieve reminded them.

"You must be joking!" Thérèse exclaimed. "I can't write."

"Yes you can," Sister Marie said firmly. "You wrote a beautiful poem about Joan of Arc, and that song 'Living For Love', and the playlet for St Martha's Feast."

"Bits and pieces, written under obedience," Thérèse objected.

163

"Then order her to write it now," Sister Marie said. "Go on, Mother."

"Very well," Mother Agnes smiled. "I order you to write an account of your life for my feast day next year. You can do it in your spare time."

Thérèse would have liked to ask in what spare time, but that would have been impertinent. Instead she said, "But what could I write about that you don't know already?"

"Write it anyway," the Prioress said. "It will be pleasant to refresh my memory about some of the things I've forgotten."

"I have a couple of old exercise books I brought with me. You may have them," Sister Génévieve offered.

"If you order it, Mother." Thérèse spoke with resignation.

It seemed like a waste of time to hark back to days that were gone. In Carmel the Sisters were not encouraged to look back at the world they had left but to settle into the new life they had chosen. Certainly, despite the order, she wouldn't feel justified in giving up any of her duties in order to write it, which meant she would have to confine her literary efforts to the hours after ten-thirty when the Grand Silence had been rung and the nuns had retired to their cells.

That same night, armed with the exercise books and pencil, she sat down at her writing desk. The cell was cold but quiet, lit by the flickering light of the lamp. A story, she supposed, would have to have a title, but she couldn't think of any. After a few moments of staring at the intimidating blank page, she took out the little volume of the Gospels which she always carried and opened it at random, hoping some stray sentence would catch her eye and provide some inspiration. The flower, brown petalled now with its root dried up, which Louis had picked for her, met her gaze. She touched its fragile stem with a gentle finger and smiled. At least she had her title.

'The Story of A Little White Flower.'

It looked rather grand, written across the top of the page. Her task now was to fill up all the other pages. Slowly she began to write.

'Dearest Mother, it is to you, who are my mother twice over that I am going to tell the story of my soul.'

After all, it was for Mother Agnes, for dearest Pauline, that she was writing, and Pauline wouldn't mind little faults of style. From some deep, inner well, memories bubbled up, shaping themselves into words and phrases. She wrote steadily, hunched over her desk, while the lamp burned fitfully and the convent settled into night.

It was not every day nor even every week that she could add to her manuscript. There were nights when her duties during the day were so heavy that she had to get them finished during the Grand Silence and it was midnight before she crept to her cell. Sometimes she had five precious minutes during the day when she could slip away to add a line or two, but such occasions were rare.

Her days were filled up with the lessons for the novices to be prepared, the sacristy to be cleaned and polished, the flower beds to be weeded, the dishes to wipe, and the obligatory attendances in choir. There was scarcely any time for her own reading and meditations, and more than once Thérèse found herself nodding off to sleep in the middle of Mass. At one time she would have been overwhelmed with guilt at such bad manners, but it occurred to her that if God allowed her to doze off in church, He probably had an excellent reason for doing so.

Meanwhile summer was approaching and her spirits rose as the birds returned and the flowers bloomed. Much as she loved snow the warm weather made her feel more cheerful and energetic. The extreme cold that still distressed her more than any of the other privations was mitigated for a few months, and she revelled in the bright sunshine and the humming of the bees as they hunted for nectar.

"You look happy, Sister Thérèse," one of the lay-sisters paused to say.

"I was watching my little rabbits." She nodded towards a small group of postulants who were chattering together in the few minutes between classes.

"You are hard enough on your rabbits," the other said sourly. "They often end up in tears when you've finished scolding them."

"A good vocation needs to be watered a little," Thérèse said, "and they know I don't mean to be unkind."

"They don't like you very much though," her companion said. "You are not generally popular, you know."

"When I am dead everybody will love me," Thérèse said.

"You seem to be very certain of it."

"Yes, quite certain, but it won't matter if they don't. Anything suits me."

Thérèse gave her smiling little nod and moved on. She had promised to take a turn in the laundry to give Sister Martha an opportunity to catch up on her meditations, and if she were not careful she would be late.

The laundry was baking hot, steam rising from the sizzling irons, the nuns pausing to wipe the sweat from their faces.

Sister Martha took off her apron and tied it about Thérèse's waist, fumbling with the safety pin that anchored it to the shoulder, driving the point deeply into her flesh.

"Thank you, Sister. Go to your meditation now." Thérèse smiled, controlling the cry of pain that had risen to her

166

lips. One of the other Sisters had glanced across, and if she moved the pin now Sister Martha would be blamed for her carelessness. Thérèse picked up the heavy iron and set to work, feeling the blood run down inside her habit, waiting until she could turn away without being observed to draw out the sharp steel.

Within a few minutes the sweat was pouring down her face. If she wiped it away one of the others would immediately offer to take her place, and herself suffer the same inconvenience for this was the hottest part of the room. Thérèse went on ironing steadily without pause, remarking when a passing Sister stopped in concern, "It is so cosy in here out of the breeze, don't you think?"

"Sister, I was very rude to you before."

The lay sister who had spoken to her in the garden approached her as she emerged from the laundry.

"You spoke the truth, Sister," Thérèse said equably. "I am not much liked. At school I was not much liked either."

"I spoke spitefully and it wasn't entirely true. Many of the Sisters admire and respect you."

"Thank you, Sister." Thérèse began to move away. She had an enormous bunch of cornflowers in water ready to be arranged at the feet of the Child Jesus. The sacristy would be cool and peaceful, a haven of tranquillity where she could refresh herself for half an hour.

"Sister, do allow me to do a little favour for you to make up for my unkindness," the other was begging.

"I would be most grateful if you could see to the flowers in the sacristy for me," Thérèse said. "There are some cornflowers to be arranged."

"I shall be delighted," the lay sister took off as if her heels had grown wings.

In the strawberry beds Sister John was on her knees,

liming a net. She glanced up, smiling as Thérèse paused.

"Wasting your time, young lady? Whenever I see you, you are strolling around doing nothing. Now why don't you help me with these?"

"Forgive me, Sister, but I can't set traps," Thérèse said. "I wish you wouldn't do it either. The poor little birds have only this life to enjoy, and their singing is so sweet."

"Child, they peck at the strawberries," Sister John explained.

"Haven't we sufficient for them?"

"It's a waste, throwing them away to sparrows," the old nun said stubbornly.

"Sister, I'll make a bargain with you." Thérèse squatted on her heels, lowering her voice. "If you promise not to snare any more birds then I promise to make sure after I'm dead to send you a big basket of fruit every year."

"I'll be dead myself by then or are you planning on leaving soon?" the other enquired.

"Oh, I don't say that I shall die in the next month or even year," Thérèse said earnestly, "but sooner than you think, and I'll make certain God sends you your fruit."

"So you'll be telling God what to do, will you?"

"I've never refused God anything," Thérèse said simply, "so when I die He won't refuse me anything."

She rose, bobbing her head in the characteristic little nod which made her look rather like a bird herself, and moved away. Slowly, grumbling at herself for an old fool, Sister John began to wind in the nets.

Thérèse toiled up the stairs to her cell. It was cool here and she rinsed her hands and face and decided there wasn't time to do any writing. She would sit down for a few moments and try to collect her thoughts.

She squatted on the stone floor, fixing her eyes on the black cross. The notice beneath questioned her.

'Daughter, what are you doing here?'

"I'm not doing anything much at all," she said aloud.

It wasn't easy to become a saint, she thought sadly. Once she had imagined it would be easy if only she got into Carmel, but it was proving very difficult. Every morning she woke up hoping that by some miracle perfection would have come upon her during the night, but by night she knew that she was nowhere near it. Yet people were expected to become saints, to be perfect. She couldn't believe that God had only chosen important spiritual leaders to partake of His glory. Heaven was meant for ordinary people, for all the little, struggling souls who wanted to be good and didn't know how to set about it. There ought to be a little way to Heaven, Thérèse thought, a way for the little souls like herself who couldn't become martyrs, or missionaries, or founders of religious Orders. What she needed was a key that would open the first door. She had no key, nothing but her love for God and her own small sacrifices to offer Him. And that was sufficient she thought. Why, St Paul himself had written that nothing was of any use without charity. Charity was only another name for love. All creation was founded on love, but people sometimes forgot that. They were so busy blaming themselves that they forgot God only wanted to be loved.

"What did you wish to see me about, Sister?" Mother Agnes asked, looking up from her desk as Thérèse tapped on the door.

"I have a favour to ask, Mother Prioress."

"Yes? What is it?" Mother Agnes frowned slightly, wondering what was coming. Her little sister never asked for privileges.

"Will you grant me this, Mother?" Thérèse handed a closely written piece of paper to her superior.

"An offering of myself as a holocaust victim to the

merciful love of God," Mother Agnes read aloud. "Sister, what is this?"

"I want to represent all the little, ordinary people," Thérèse said. "There are martyrs who are victims of God's Justice, so why shouldn't there be a victim of His love. Why not? A love so pure, so searing, that it burns you up if you fling yourself into it."

"We cannot all feel love like that," Mother Agnes began.

"Then I shall feel it for other people," Thérèse said, clasping her hands tightly. "I never did manage to do anything important or useful, Mother, but I can love. That doesn't take great talent or heroism. All you have to do is to love. Love and do your best. It's so simple!"

"A victim of Divine Love. It's a strange notion and might be misunderstood," Mother Agnes said.

"Everybody loves someone at some time in their lives," Thérèse argued. "Oh, please let me do this on behalf of all the people who don't know how to love or don't have anybody. Please!"

"Very well. I'll read it and you may—offer yourself," Mother Agnes said slowly. "Go to the chapel and pray about it."

Thérèse went at her usual serene pace, but her heart was hammering. She hadn't been so excited since the day of her Clothing, but this was subtly different for she knew now the direction that her path would take. She might not be able to die in the arena or convert pagans, but she could love and try every second to please her Beloved in small ways that nobody else would notice.

The little chapel was empty with only the red sanctuary lamp glowing softly. She sank to her knees, taking up her long, black rosary. It was a pity that the Rosary was the most boring form of devotion that she knew. For that reason she always made a point of saying each prayer slowly and carefully as if her life depended on it. At least God would be aware that she was trying her best. Prayers were like love letters. Not everyone who wrote a love letter could write great literature, but it was the loving that mattered.

The prayers finished and the usual over-mastering desire for sleep having been conquered, she rose. There was just time to make the Stations of the Cross before Vespers. Later on, if she was fortunate, there would be time to do a little writing.

The shaft of fire struck through to the source of her being as she glanced up at the altar. It was a fire that burned without pain, an intensity of concentrated passion that pierced her with intolerable sweetness. The air was fragrant, whirling with colours she had never even imagined existed. She thought for a moment that she had already died and been snatched up to Heaven, but already the fire was cooling and she was standing, bathed in sweat, her mind desperately trying to catch at the experience and hold it but it had gone like a dream, and there was nothing left in her but a sick, grey, tired feeling.

She would be twenty-three the following year. If her premonition was wrong she might live in this enclosure for another fifty or sixty years and at the end, there might be nothing but an eternity of darkness. There might not be an after life after all, nothing but nothingness.

For a minute the possibility crushed her and she stood with bowed head, fighting the worst temptation of her life. She waited, but the grey apathy that had descended upon her intensified until there was nothing within her but an aching loss for something that might not even exist.

But loving was a reality. It was the only reality she had. Even if there was nothing beyond that she wouldn't abandon the way that she had chosen.

FOURTEEN

Her childhood reminiscences had been finished and laid before Mother Agnes. Thérèse had not bothered to enquire her opinion of them. Indeed by the end she had been writing as much for herself as for anyone else. It was satisfying to put thoughts on paper, to examine the child she had been—in many ways a very foolish, spoiled child, she thought ruefully. But she had written as honestly as she could, and her task done had returned to her duties.

Life held none of the spiritual consolations she had hoped to find in the peace and quiet of Carmel. She felt that she moved in an arid desert where there was no refreshment for the soul, nothing to lift the grey apathy that wrapped her round as closely as the cloth that Papa had once shrouded his head in. What she wanted to achieve was so very much more than she managed to achieve, that when she examined her conscience at the end of each day she could only find to say in her own mitigation that she had always tried to do her best. It was as much as anyone could do, and she consoled herself with that.

She had other duties now. Mother Agnes had given her the names of two young missionary priests with instructions to write to them, encouraging them in their vocations, advising them in their moments of doubt and depression.

"The pot calling the kettle black," she said aloud in the privacy of her cell, and laughed as she penned solemn words of advice for her spiritual brothers. How startled Father Belliére and Father Roulland would be if they ever found out that their mentor was a girl of twenty-three who was herself not even sure that Heaven existed!

Although she was careful to confine her letters to religious subjects, she looked forward eagerly to the correspondence that arrived from them. Their descriptions of the work they did on their mission stations opened vistas in her imagination. Lands she had never seen, peopled by men and women in strange clothes speaking unintelligible languages, crowded her mind. She had always enjoyed geography lessons at school and now she pored over a coloured map, trying to picture what it would be like to live out there. To be a missionary Sister seemed to her to be the highest calling to which anyone could aspire.

In the spring there were elections again for the Prioress, and despite her determination to remain aloof Thérèse couldn't help a pang of disappointment when Mother Marie Gonsague gained the majority.

"By a very narrow margin," she said with commendable honesty. "It was a very grave disappointment to me. This is a divided Carmel, I fear."

"Oh, no, Mother!" Thérèse looked up in distress. "Those who didn't vote for you will accept the view of the rest and extend to you a similar love and obedience."

"And will you, now that Sister Agnes will be back in the laundry?" Mother Marie de Gonsague asked.

"I have no vote in Chapter," Thérèse reminded her. "I give my duty where it is required of me."

"You're cold hearted," the Prioress complained. "Your own sisters crave more of your company than you give them. You know, of course, that your cousin, Marie Guérin, is to join us here?"

"Uncle Isidore came to tell us." Thérèse's eyes brightened. "I have prayed so hard that Cousin Marie would come. She has wanted to take the veil for a long time, but my uncle and aunt had very natural doubts."

"You can scarcely be said to have abandoned your family when you came in here," the Prioress said dryly.

"It troubles me," Thérèse said frankly. "My sisters are here and Cousin Marie is entering, and I've known many of the nuns since I was a child. To go among strangers unbound by any ties of natural affection is far more of a sacrifice. I have a very easy time of it here."

"Your troubles may soon be over," Mother Marie de Gonsague said. "I have heard from our foundation in Saigon, in Indochina. They want to found another Carmel in Hanoi, and they are asking for a nun to be sent out to help in its establishment. I am going to put forward your name."

"To go to Indochina?" Thérèse spoke in breathless excitement.

"Provided your health can stand the long journey and the climate."

"I've never felt better!" Thérèse exclaimed.

"You look well enough," the other said grudgingly. "I will write to inform them of my decision. Meanwhile you may begin your preparations for the task ahead. You will require to learn something of the customs and history of the country, of course. You will have to find time during your recreation for that. Don't forget that your duties here still bind you. What occupation do you have?"

"Whatever nobody else happens to be doing at the time," Thérèse said.

"A flippant reply from a professed religious! What exactly have you done today for instance?"

"After breakfast I cleaned out the sacristy and mended some of the altar linen," Thérèse said, knitting her brow slightly. "Then I planted some flowers, and hung out the laundry, and then I had a class with the postulants, and then I peeled the potatoes and then I——"

"There is no need to go on so, Sister!" the Prioress said irritably. "I could show you half a dozen nuns who do twice as much with half as much fuss! You will certainly have the leisure to study conditions in Indochina. I intend to confirm you in your position as assistant Novice Mistress, but I will retain the office of Novice Mistress myself as well as that of Prioress. Did you say something, Sister?"

She would have liked to say a great deal, but she merely smiled, saying placidly,

"No, Mother Prioress, I didn't speak."

"You may go then. Try to be a little more useful for the rest of the day."

"Yes, Mother Prioress."

Poor Mother Marie de Gonsague. Thérèse felt immense pity for the prickly, difficult woman who clung so tenaciously to her privileges. Yet she had fine qualities if only she could overcome her personal defects, her emotional instability and jealousy of the Martins.

'And I have no right to harbour such thoughts about Mother Prioress,' she told herself sternly. 'Oh, but Pauline was a fine one, and she deserves a better occupation than laundry work. And that's an extra decade of the rosary for you, Sister Thérèse, for losing your detachment! It will be very good for Pauline's soul to carry heavy baskets of washing around. Really, it's high time I was torn away from my relatives. I cannot help worrying about them. But to go to Hanoi! Dear Lord, but You give me so much for which to be grateful. To live in a country that's warm, among people who don't know me as Thérèse Martin—oh, I shall work so hard to make You loved among the pagans!"

Word of her going to Indochina filtered along the Carmelite grapevine. If her sisters grieved at the prospect of her going abroad, perhaps for ever, they generously gave no sign of their feelings, and she found herself deluged with congratulations and advice.

"You will have to learn how to eat with chopsticks," Sister Généviève teased.

"And pick rice!" Mother Agnes said.

"I shall wear a big flat straw hat," Thérèse said happily, "and my skin will burn as brown as a berry!"

She was happier than she had been for months at the prospect of the adventure. Even the thought of leaving her sisters was no more than the salt that gave savour to the dish. No matter how hard she tried to efface herself at Lisieux she was still little Thérèse Martin. It would strengthen her to be in a place where her background was previously unknown.

She listened with deep attention when Father Pichon, returned recently from the Canadian Mission, talked of the particular qualities needed by a missionary Sister.

"There are still parts of the world where it is dangerous to be a Christian, still places where it is possible to be martyred, though we don't encourage our Sisters to fling themselves into danger. A cool head and an iron nerve are both essential, spiced with commonsense."

'And love,' Thérèse thought. 'Loving is more important than anything.' She wrote at once to Father Roulland at Sut-Chien to give him her news. It would be agreeable if he could make shift to come and meet her. Not that she expected, or even hoped, for special treatment but Indo-china was very far from home, and it was pleasant to think she might have the opportunity of thanking him for the interest that his letters gave her.

That night, her letter already speeding on its way, she lay down to sleep with a happier smile on her face than she had worn in private for months. It was Holy Thursday

177

and she had taken her turn at kneeling before the exposed Host with the conviction that the greyness was lifting and her true mission about to begin.

Without warning a flood of something warm and salty filled her mouth and she groped in the darkness for her handkerchief, longing to relight her lamp and find out what had happened. The relighting of one's lamp was forbidden save in dire emergency, and Thérèse couldn't honestly class herself as an emergency. She had tasted blood and the thought that she might be dying ran through her with a curious thrill that was part dread and part anticipation. Well, if she was, she could do it equally properly in the dark as in the light. Crumpling her handkerchief, she lay down again and fell asleep as quickly as a child.

Morning brought confirmation of her suspicion. She stared at the bright stain that had soaked through the handkerchief. It was Good Friday and the knowledge brought with it a joy so intense that her whole being glowed.

Mother Marie de Gonsague, wearied after a night's vigil in the chapel, regarded the small figure before her with some disfavour. God forgive her, but she could not look at Sister Thérèse of the Child Jesus without feeling intensely irritated.

"What is it, Sister?"

"I spat this up last night, Mother Prioress."

Thérèse held out the stained handkerchief.

"Are you sick?" Mother Marie de Gonsague peered first at the handkerchief and then at the pale faced supplicant.

"I don't have any pain," Thérèse said.

"Are you asking to be excused from the penances of this solemn feast day?"

"No, Mother Prioress, but I felt it was my duty to inform you."

"Are you asking for a doctor?"

"No, Mother Prioress."

"And you don't feel yourself to be in any immediate danger."

"Not in the least, Mother."

"You had an ulcer in your throat some months ago. It's probable that it's burst," the Prioress said. "It will mean a disappointment for you."

"Hanoi?"

"They will expect me to provide them with a healthy nun, not one given to ulcerated throats," the Prioress said, drumming her fingers. "This is too unfortunate! I hoped— well, hope is delusive. We cannot risk sending you on a long journey during which you might fall ill, and I really don't like the idea of your becoming a burden on the Community out there."

"I don't wish to be a burden anywhere," Thérèse ventured.

"But it's inevitable that you will. Well, it is partly my own fault for taking you in at so early an age," the older woman fretted. "I don't know what to do about you!"

"I'm not in any pain," Thérèse repeated.

"Then I suggest you continue your usual duties," the Prioress said at last. "I will ask you again how you feel in a month or two. Remember that we are here to embrace suffering. I would have no time left for anything else if all my nuns came running to me every time they had some little ailment."

"Thank you, Mother Prioress." Thérèse genuflected and went out. It was true that she was not in pain but she did feel very exhausted, as if all her energy had drained out of her.

She had already been set her Good Friday task, and she went to it without delay, collecting the two pails of water that would be used for the washing of the windows.

179

"Sister Thérèse, you don't look well. Shall I wash the windows?"

One of her novices had paused to speak to her.

"Have you finished your own task?"

"Yes, Sister."

"Then go and help Sister John. She is sweeping the paths and her rheumatism is very bad," Thérèse said.

"But you look very pale," the other said anxiously.

"I will sunbathe later in the year," Thérèse said. "Go along now, for we are both wasting time."

Summer was still months away and it would be spent at Lisieux, not in the heat of Indochina among the bamboo shoots and the rice and the smiling, slant-eyed pagans. She would never have the joy of seeing a convert baptized or of telling tales from the Bible for the children of the Mission. It would be unfair to be a burden on the Community. Mother Prioress was right not to send her, but it didn't make the disappointment any the less bitter. Despite her efforts to look on the cheerful side of this latest disaster, she couldn't prevent a few scalding tears falling into the bucket of water.

"You are certain you're fit to carry on?" Mother Marie de Gonsague lowered her voice as she gave Thérèse the goodnight salute.

"Yes, Mother Prioress." Thérèse gave her usual serene smile.

In a few minutes she would be safe in the privacy of her cell. Then she would be able to cry without being noticed. Except by God. God would notice and be disappointed because she had let Him down, moaning and weeping instead of rejoicing because she had been asked to make a little sacrifice.

After all she had longed with all her heart for the opportunity to enter Carmel and now, after only eight years, she was restless, wanting to be off travelling the world, meeting new people, seeing some results of her prayers. She was unfit to be a Carmelite, but for some reason God had made it possible for her to become one. So she might as well be as good a one as she could, given her limited talents and imperfect nature.

She dashed the tears from her eyes and undressed slowly, folding her habit neatly, kissing her cross and her discipline before laying them on her writing table.

She was drifting off to sleep when, between dream and reality, she was aware that she was sitting up, rising from her narrow bed, walking down a long, high gallery. There were figures standing there, veiled and silent, but she had the impression that they were watching her. Then a tall Carmelite, veiled like the others, stepped forward and, lifting her veil, threw it over Thérèse. She recognized the tall woman with the calm, beautiful face without knowing how she did so as the Venerable Anne of Jesus who had brought the first Carmelites to France, and cried out in surprise and pleasure, "Am I coming to Heaven soon?"

"Very soon," the Venerable Anne said and her smile was warm.

"But I do so little!" Thérèse was moved to protest. "Is God content with such small sacrifices? Doesn't He want more from me?"

"Dear child, He is happy with you just as you are," the other replied.

She wanted to ask for some favours for the other Sisters, but the veiled, shimmering figures were withdrawing, the gallery shrinking into a cell again.

It was dawn, but the darkness was thicker than it had ever been. There was more blood spotting her handkerchief and a dull pain in her chest. The dream was clear in her mind, but it was no more than a dream now, and all she

FIFTEEN

"I ought to have been called in a year ago," Dr de Cornières had said, his voice tight with impotent fury. "Have you no idea of the difference between an ulcerated throat and pulmonary tuberculosis?"

"Sister Thérèse made no complaint," Mother Marie de Gonsague said wretchedly. "She has simply carried out her normal duties. Nobody could have guessed there was anything wrong with her."

"We will try everything possible." The physician snapped shut his bag. "Cod-liver oil, blistering, mercury treatment—they will prolong her life for a few months. I always said that little girl wasn't long for this world."

It was no longer possible for her to carry out all her duties, though on the days that she felt a little better she went to the laundry or the kitchens as usual. But there were days when she had to lie on the wheeled couch under the chestnut trees and occupy herself with sewing and writing.

She had written a long essay for Sister Marie trying to explain the simple philosophy of living at which she had arrived, and now Mother Marie de Gonsague had ordered her to go on with her reminscences.

"Write more of your spiritual progress," she said. "The novices tell me that you talk to them about your little way to Heaven. Write about that."

She had written steadily, a little every day, throughout the summer. Words flowed out and her only difficulties lay in the frequent interruptions she was called on to

183

endure when the other Sisters stopped for a few words.

"You should rest, Sister," Mother Agnes said, pausing to frown at Thérèse.

"I like to write," Thérèse said, smiling up at her. "Truly it's no work at all, Mother!"

"We may have you with us for a long time yet." The elder tried to look hopeful. "Perhaps you've reached the turning point and you'll begin to recover now."

"It would be nice to recover," Thérèse said, her blue eyes wistful, "but I've been thinking that perhaps some people reach old age when they are very young. Time is only a word after all."

"Mother Prioress has been more harsh with you than any of us!"

"Perhaps with reason. Life might have been too easy for me otherwise. I was always very spoiled and wilful," Thérèse said ruefully.

"Don't work too hard," Mother Agnes said as she moved away.

She meant to be kind, Thérèse thought with a sigh. Nobody knew how painful it was to draw breath, or how the open blisters on her side bled every time she moved. At night her fever mounted so high that she felt as if she were burning up, and during the day such fits of trembling ran through her that she found it almost impossible to stand upright. Heaven, if it existed, must surely be better than this constant physical torment.

"I am not a great saint," she said thoughtfully when they came to help her into chapel. "I am only a little saint. After I am dead they will try to make out that I was great and noble, but you must tell them I was just a little saint for ordinary people to follow. Nothing more than that."

"Mother Prioress talks of having your writings privately

184

printed for distribution among the Carmels of France," Mother Agnes said.

"Oh, that will do a great deal of good," Thérèse said eagerly. "People would be able to read all about my faults and temptations then, and they would understand that it doesn't matter. It is loving that counts. Loving until we are swallowed up in Love."

"Don't set your heart on it," Sister Génévieve warned. "Mother Prioress changes her mind so often that she is just as likely to throw the lot on the fire."

"It won't matter. I shall find some other way of getting my message to everybody," Thérèse assured her.

"When you get to Heaven you will be reunited with God and be able to rest," Mother Agnes said consolingly.

"No, indeed I won't," Thérèse said firmly. "I will be exceedingly busy when I get to Heaven, doing all the things I couldn't do on earth. That will be my mission."

"If you're a saint it's probable you'll remain incorrupt. Many do," Sister Marie said.

"Only very important saints. Dig me up and you'll find a little skeleton," Thérèse said.

They had reached the chapel and she sank to her knees, composing herself for the service. The aridity was total now. She could hope for no gleam of light to pierce the thick veil of doubt. If God existed anywhere then He was asleep. If He didn't exist then she had spent twenty-four years loving an illusion. It didn't trouble her unduly for the act of loving was a fact that nothing could destroy. Kindness and gaiety were realities and everything else was a hope springing from them.

She had time to pick up some litter before supper. The Mother Prioress had told her nine years before to pick it up until further notice and, as she had never rescinded her order, Thérèse had continued with the task. She moved slowly, bending to pick up the odd scraps of paper that lay about. From the refectory window Sister Vincent's voice floated out.

"They say Sister Thérèse of the Child Jesus is going to die soon. I wonder what on earth they'll find to say about her in the Obituary, for she has never done anything worth talking about!"

"She's a good little thing," another voice objected.

"Well, she doesn't get any merits for practising virtue," Sister Vincent retorted crossly. "It comes naturally to her."

Thérèse allowed herself a wry little smile before she went her way.

There was so much more that she wanted to write about, her pencil raced over the paper as if it had a will of its own.

"I'm certain that if my conscience were burdened with all the sins it's possible to commit I would still fly to Him on the wings of confidence and of love——"

The pencil dropped from her fingers and rolled a little way across the grass. There was so much more to say, but she was dripping with sweat and every breath was an agony.

It was no longer possible for her to go out into the garden. Instead, propped up in the infirmary, she watched the blue sky beyond the window. It was late July and so hot that she found it hard to remember how she had once suffered from the cold. It was no longer possible for her to carry out her duties or even to attend services in the chapel. There was nothing left to be done but get on with the task of dying as cheerfully as possible. Everybody was being very kind. Even Mother Marie de Gonsague's sharp sarcasms were quieted. Mother Agnes and Sister Marie took it in turns to sleep in the little room next to the infirmary, but their determined attempts to be hopeful and encourag-

186

ing worried her dreadfully. She knew they suffered to see her suffer, and it was not always possible to hide it now. Even the rustling of a leaf pounded through her head, and the perfume of the flowers in the vase at her bedside made her nose bleed.

"I will send down a shower of roses when I'm dead," she informed them.

Her novices came to see her every day, even though they had rebelled against her strictness. She wished they would go away and leave her in peace, but that would have been unkind, so she roused herself to listen to their troubles and tease them out of their moods of gloom.

The statue that had once smiled at her in the bedroom of Les Buissonets had been brought to the convent and placed at the foot of her bed. It was a kind gesture, but there was only the statue there now.

It was no longer possible for her to eat and drink without vomiting, and the darkness around was so impenetrable that she wondered whether it was a foretaste of an eternal darkness to come. Well, she could go on loving in darkness.

"Do keep my possessions carefully," she managed to gasp. "People will want them when I am dead. They will want even my nail clippings."

She was only a little ordinary saint but at least she could die with courage. Joan of Arc had died with courage, but she had suffered for only twenty minutes in the fire and Thérèse had been in the infirmary for nearly two months.

"I envy you," Sister Teresa of St Augustine said, "to be so certain of going to Heaven."

Sister Teresa was a pious fool, Thérèse thought, but it would do her no good to tell her so.

"I am not even certain there is a Heaven, or life after death," she was moved to confide, "but if there is then I shall come back and let you know."

187

"You know I've often wondered why you've always sought my company so often," Sister Teresa remarked. "What is it about me that pleases you so much?"

Dear Sister Teresa who rattled her rosary beads in chapel until Thérèse wanted to scream and whose well-meant kindness set her teeth on edge!

"It is you who pleases me," she said ambiguously and was almost glad that a fit of coughing made it impossible for her to enlarge on the matter.

"There's so much to be done," she said to Sister Généviève, "and yet I can do nothing until I'm dead, except lie here being a burden! It's so unfair on the rest of you!"

"I don't know how we will bear it without you," Sister Généviève said brokenly.

"Oh, you will be so busy after I'm gone," Thérèse assured her, "that you'll have no time to grieve."

But it was becoming harder and harder to speak, hard even to swallow or even to move. She could only sob weakly to Mother Agnes,

"I can't endure much more. If you only knew! Dying is a terrible thing."

Somewhere in the convent the great bell was tolling. That must mean she was very near to the end. But the echoes of the bell died, and the hours passed, and she was still breathing. She could hear each rasping breath and feel the bed shaking beneath her.

It was growing darker outside and her Sisters had come in with candles in their hands. Somewhere a clock struck seven.

"Is it time to go yet?" she managed to breathe.

"It may last for several hours yet," the Mother Prioress said.

All her life everything had been delayed. All her life

nothing had happened at the moment she wanted it.

"Right then. Let's go on." She set her teeth against the spasm of agony, her face purpling. She had heard such edifying stories of how beautifully the great saints had died, of the visions they had had, but she was only an ordinary saint. She didn't have anything left except the reality of her own loving.

She called out suddenly in a clear voice that rang through the room in triumph. "I love!"

"Sister?" Mother Agnes moved her candle nearer to the astonished blue eyes and mouth opened in joyful welcome.

"Sister?"

But Thérèse had begun her mission.

EPILOGUE

1959

In April she would be ninety years old. When she took time to think about it the fact astonished her. Inside she still felt quite young and vigorous, and her memory was phenomenal, as some of the naughtier postulants found out to their cost when they tried to wriggle out of their duties.

But it was a little sad to be the only one left out of all the family who could remember the old days. Aunt Elisa had survived Thérèse by only three years and then poor Cousin Marie had died and then Uncle Isidore, and only Cousin Jeanne, widowed and devoting herself to charitable works, had been left on the outside to endure the first Great War.

That had been a terrible time, delaying the investigation by the authorities into Thérèse's life and work. Mother Marie de Gonsague had sent the little book round to all the other Carmels and they had lent it out to their relatives and friends, and in no time at all they were being besieged from all over the world for copies. Since then the book had sold in millions, and thousands of people had travelled to Lisieux to demand relics and photographs of the unknown nun whose simple philosophy had touched their hearts. Little ordinary people, the old nun thought, who knew only how to love. That would have pleased Thérèse, but there was no doubt she knew about it. Thérèse was enjoying an industrious eternity, appearing all over the world, sending down mysterious showers of roses, the scent of violets and lilies, ceaselessly busy. There had been a demand for the recognition of her sanctity that swelled into a roar until Rome had been forced to listen.

And now she was Saint Thérèse, Patroness of France and Patroness of Missions, the most powerful and popular saint of modern times, her words translated into every known language, her relics lovingly preserved, the places where she had lived or visited become places of pilgrimage. But in the quietness of Carmel, they were shielded against the worst excesses of popular acclaim. Here they could live the hidden life, unknown, unguessed at by the souvenir hunters.

And they had long lives, she thought. Léonie had returned to the Visitation Convent and persevered in her vocation, dying when she was two years short of eighty. Dear, quirky Léonie with her fits of generosity and her wry humour.

"I belong to a family of saints and I am hoping not to let down the side," she had written a few weeks before her death.

Marie had lived to be eighty and died at the start of the second and more dreadful war, but the two remaining had lived through the German occupation and the bombardment of Lisieux and the uneasy peace. She had thought the soldiers with their boys' faces and tired eyes had been touching in their eagerness to have a photograph of the "Cute little saint."

Mother Agnes had been made Prioress for life eventually and died at the age of ninety, hiding the severe pain of her illness just as her little sister had done, burdened by the constant stream of visitors to be interviewed, photographs to sign, letters to answer.

Now she was the only one left, the only one who could remember the old days, before they had entered the religious life, when they had all been together at Les

Buissonets with Papa and Victoire.

Papa and Mamma had both been officially beatified. The Martins were the most famous family in Normandy, all saints perpetually on their knees if one believed the guide-books, but she could remember when they had just been Céline and Thérèse, playing with their dolls.

"What are you going to be when you are a big girl, Thérèse?"

"A saint," the little girl had shrilled, wobbling on one leg.

Thérèse, Sister Généviève thought, had always been a very determined little girl. A smile lifted the corners of her mouth at the vivid memories that crowded her mind.

"Sister, look what has come up in the garden, in all this ice and snow!" one of the novices exclaimed, pointing through the window.

It was white petalled, sheathed in green leaves, pushing its way bravely into a winter world.

"It's the sign of my going," Sister Généviève said slowly.

After that there would be nobody else left. Nobody, except the snow blossom. It was enough.

The End